DIRTY LITTLE PROMISE

Forbidden Desires, Book Two

KENDALL RYAN

Dirty Little Promise
Copyright © 2017 Kendall Ryan

Copy Editing and Formatting by
Pam Berehulke

Cover Design by
Okay Creations

All rights reserved. No part of this book may be reproduced or transmitted in any form without written permission of the author, except by a reviewer who may quote brief passages for review purposes only.

This book is a work of fiction. Names, characters, places, and incidents are either the product of the author's imagination or are used fictitiously.

About the Book

Conflicted by the depth of her feelings for bad boy Gavin Kingsley, lonely librarian Emma Bell knows he's all wrong for her—yet the heart wants what it wants.

But if she gives in to his dark, erotic desires, will she lose herself completely?

Passion, drama, and suspense combine in the highly anticipated conclusion to Gavin and Emma's love affair. This is book two in the intoxicating Forbidden Desires series.

Chapter One

Gavin

Son of a bitch.

I slammed down the phone and squeezed my eyes closed with a sigh.

A second girl had called out of work tonight, and there was nothing I could do except grin and bear it. After all, it wasn't like I could fill in as the sexy arm candy for some wealthy CEO looking for a date. Truthfully, I knew it shouldn't upset me so much. In fact, it normally wouldn't. But between girls flaking out on their duties and Cooper not showing up for work today, I was nearly at my wit's end.

And then there was Emma. Sexy, gorgeous Emma who was supposed to fly with me tonight to Florida for a weekend golf outing. Except, of course, she hadn't answered my calls for nearly a week.

A fucking *week*. I'd been slammed at work, and maybe she'd been busy too, but this was ridiculous.

Emma was unlike anyone else I'd ever met. If there was one person who wasn't afraid to do what she wanted, regardless of the consequences, it was my sexy little librarian. That still didn't explain what had happened to make her run in the opposite direction.

We'd shared some hot nights together, and one amazing afternoon in the library where she worked. It had all been going so well . . . felt so right. I'd even opened up to her a little and told her about my past.

Then, just like that?

Poof.

She was gone. Ghosting me for some unknown reason.

Slowly, I pulled my hand into a fist, cracking each of my knuckles until they let out a little pop. Then I let out a long sigh.

I could try calling her again. It would be the third time today—a desperate move that wasn't like me—but I had to know if she was coming with me tonight as promised. I was thinking over my options as a gentle knock sounded on my door.

"Come in," I muttered, a little more gruffly than I'd

intended.

Our hiring manager, Sonja, stepped into the office, her sleek frame wrapped in a crimson dress and her blond hair swirled into an elegant knot at the nape of her neck. She batted her extended eyelashes at me as I glanced up in question, waiting for whatever it was she'd come to say.

"I'm sorry to bother you, Gavin," Sonja said, her voice soft and husky.

"No bother. Just a long day." I motioned to the leather chair across from my desk and she followed my instruction, setting her pile of folders on my desk. "What's going on?"

"I thought you might want to talk about bringing on some new girls. I've noticed that Alyssa has been frustrated, and wondered if there was something else we should do to weed out candidates who aren't pulling their weight, or only want to work when it pleases them." She grinned and crossed her legs, sending her skirt slinking up one toned thigh. "You're always good for bouncing these ideas off of, so I thought I'd pop in."

I stared at her blankly, not sure how to respond. The

compliment was a little out of left field since I rarely got involved in such matters, but given the calls Alyssa had been fielding today, I wasn't about to turn Sonja away.

"Thank you for noticing. Let me see what you have."

I held out my hand and she passed me the folders, her thumb brushing my palm before she moved her hand away. I frowned, staring at where she'd touched me very deliberately, but then shook my head as I opened the first file.

The girl was pretty enough. She'd come to Boston to be an actress, and every inch of her face showed it. She smiled too wide, her eyes too open. Even in the photo, I could tell she was acting.

"I like her." I nodded, pushing past my irritation. "Call her and see if she can fill in for one of our no-shows tonight. If she can, get her paperwork done and get her out there."

Sonja nodded, taking the folder I handed back to her and pausing to jot a note on it. "Absolutely. So that's a yes on Linda Gristle."

"Linda Gristle? What a terrible name," I said,

wincing. "Give her a stage name, at least for the last bit. Cassidy. Or Miller. Something easy, but yeah, she's a go. Who else?"

"And this next one, I think she's a natural. Check it out."

I opened the next folder and glanced down. If Linda Gristle looked like she was trying too hard, this woman looked like she'd never tried a day in her life. Her demeanor didn't come off as miserable or cold, though. She just looked . . . effortless. Like someone had snapped the picture of her while she was going about her day and she'd simply happened to look incredible with copper curls and bright green eyes. On any other day, I'd have expected that face to hit me straight behind the zipper, but as pretty as she was, all I could think was that she didn't have the sex appeal that Emma had.

I flipped the manila folder shut and slid it back across the desk. "This one is an absolute yes. Call her too. We have more than one opening tonight."

"And this one?" Sonja nodded toward the last of the three folders, her posture stiffening as a strange tension filled the air.

Now wary, I opened the folder and found a picture of Sonja herself staring back at me, her blond hair hanging loosely around her heart-shaped face as she grinned, flashing her bright white teeth at the camera.

"No way," I said firmly.

She uncrossed her legs and leaned forward, her ample cleavage on full display. "I wouldn't be available to everyone. I was just thinking about your deal with Emma . . . it might be good to have someone else on retainer. You know, in case you and Cooper have an event on the same day and you need a backup?"

I pursed my lips and bit back a sharp retort. The one thing I didn't need today was a reminder of my deal with Emma. Ever since I'd left my business card at that coffee shop for her to find, she'd been invading my thoughts night and day. Then, to add insult to injury, I'd made the ingenious decision to keep myself from getting in too deep by denying my feelings for her and sharing her with my brother as our exclusive professional escort.

What a dumb fuck.

If Sonja thought she could *assist* Cooper and me in that way, quite frankly, she was delusional.

"No way." I snapped the folder shut, and the hurt in her expression made me swallow a groan.

"Is it my hair? I can wear it down." She reached for the knot at the back of her neck, and I held up a hand to stop her.

"No." I raked a hand over my face and tried to keep my blood pressure from rising any higher. I didn't want to hurt her feelings, but her timing was awful. "Look, Sonja, you're just as beautiful as any of the girls we hire as escorts, but we need to keep you where you're needed most, which is right here in this office. Complicating things by bringing you to events and charity functions . . . it'd be bad for business."

She rolled her tongue over her bottom lip as she stared at the corner of my office, her brow creased. "Right, okay. That makes sense."

"Truly, it's nothing personal."

"I believe you. And I won't badger you about it

again." She got up but didn't take the folder from in front of me. "But hang on to that just in case. The offer stays on the table."

She tucked the other two files under her arm and made for the door, her hips swaying as she walked. She paused in the doorway and turned to look at me over her shoulder, a strange darkness clouding her eyes.

"At least tell me you'll think about it?" she asked, that breathiness returning to her voice.

"Sure, fine," I said, if only because I couldn't think of anything else to say. I needed her here in the office, and pissing her off by turning her down flat wouldn't help anything. Still, as she snapped the door shut behind her, I stared after her, her words rolling around in my head.

She was thinking about the deal I'd had with Emma? I couldn't help but wonder if she had somehow found out that Emma hadn't been calling me back, and figured she'd make a play for her spot.

Racking my brain, I tried to think of a time I might have led Sonja on or given some indication that I was interested in more than just banter, but nothing came to mind. To me, she was just another employee like my assistant, Alyssa. The fact that they were women was immaterial to me.

But then, if I thought about it more . . .

Hadn't Sonja said something a few weeks ago? That she was always here when or if I needed her?

And the breathiness in her voice. That was new.

Pushing the thought away, I grabbed her file and shoved it in my bottom drawer, hoping the issue would go away before I had to solve it more aggressively. The last thing I needed was extra drama in my life.

Speaking of which . . .

Picking up the receiver, I dialed Emma's number and waited as it rang. Once, twice, three times . . . There was a click, and a second later, a flat robotic voice came over the line.

"The person you're calling has reached the maximum number of messages in their voice mail. Please call back later."

"Fuck." I grunted, then slammed down the phone

and glanced at the clock. I had to tell the charter company to start prepping the private plane soon, and I couldn't do that until I knew whether I'd be traveling alone. Growing more irritated by the second, I racked my brain until, finally, an idea popped into my head.

If Emma hadn't texted me back three days ago to tell me she was fine and just busy, I would have sent out a search party by now. But desperate times, and all that shit.

Pressing the buzzer on the corner of my desk, I said, "Alyssa, would you come in here, please?"

Within seconds, my door clicked open and Alyssa appeared wearing a navy-blue sweater dress and her dark hair in a bun much like Sonja's.

"What's going on?" she asked, her eyes wary. "Don't tell me another no-show?"

"No, thank God," I said. "I need you to do me a favor."

She shrugged. "Of course."

"It's a weird one," I warned.

She rolled her eyes. "Of course it is. But if you're

Dirty Little Promise 13

asking, it's got to be important, so shoot. What do you need me to do?"

I took a deep breath. "I need you to call Emma for me."

"For?" She raised her eyebrows.

The fact that I had to admit that Emma had been blowing me off only made me angrier, but I pushed aside my embarrassment. Frankly, I was starting to get worried about her. "She hasn't been answering my calls, and she's supposed to come with me tonight to an event in Florida. I need to get the plane prepped. And I need to make sure she's okay," I added gruffly.

I hadn't allowed myself to consider that something had happened to her. Not really, but the longer it took to hear back—and now, with her voice-mail box full—I couldn't deny a low-level sense of unrest that was growing by the minute.

"Right." Alyssa nodded, and though she didn't add anything else, I could tell she had an opinion she was holding back, which was fine with me. I wasn't in any mood to hear it.

Fishing her phone from her pocket, she entered her pass code and then passed it to me. "You know her number, I'm guessing?"

I nodded, then dialed before handing it back to her.

"What are you doing?" she asked, her hands up in defense.

"I'm not going to talk to her from your phone. That's creepy."

Alyssa scoffed at me. "*That's* the creepy part?"

I glared at her until she sighed and took the phone from me.

"Fine. Anything for you, boss."

"That's why you're the best assistant in the city."

"That's also why I need a raise."

She pressed the green dial button and held the phone to her ear, grimacing at me. Distantly, I could hear the phone ring, and then—

"Emma? Hi, it's Alyssa from Forbidden Desires."

The relief that shot through me was quickly followed by anger, and I leaned forward on my desk, my muscles bunched with tension.

After a pause, Alyssa said, "I'm well. How are you?"

When the next pause dragged out, my pulse started to hammer. "Tell me what she's saying."

Alyssa glared at me and waved me off before continuing. "Good, good. Look, I know you're really busy with the library, but we were just calling to see if you could make it to the charity golf event in Florida. We need to prime the plane and—"

A heavier silence ensued before Alyssa turned wide eyes on me. "Oh? You can't make it? That's a shame. Well—"

Waving a hand to get her attention, I ground out, "We're not taking no for an answer."

Alyssa shrugged at me helplessly and held her hand over the receiver. "What do you want me to do? Hold a gun to her head?"

"Yes," I barked.

She rolled her eyes again, then said into the phone, "Look, if you don't mind my asking, we've had some trouble getting in touch with you this week. Is everything okay?"

Blood thundering in my ears, I finally snapped and snatched the phone from Alyssa's unresisting grip. "Where have you been, pet? What's going on?"

"Gavin . . ." Emma's voice broke through, but I could tell by her tone, I wasn't going to like what she had to say. "Cooper. He told me about . . . Ashley."

My office tilted sideways, and I had to thrust out a steadying hand to my desk to keep from falling over.

She knows.

And Cooper was the one to betray me.

Fuck.

This wasn't a conversation we could have over the phone, and certainly not with Alyssa standing across from me with her hand on her hip.

"I'll be at your place in half an hour." I ended the call without waiting for Emma's reply, then handed the phone back to Alyssa.

My assistant looked at me with wide eyes. "Well, that was smooth."

"Go back to work. You have a job to do."

And so did I.

Chapter Two

Emma

What a freaking day.

Trudging home six blocks with a bundle of books under my arm, I blew a wisp of hair from my face. I'd spent the morning waiting in line at a bookstore to meet one of my favorite authors only to have her be rude and indignant, sending me away with a flick of her wrist and an overpriced paperback with my name spelled wrong.

It had been a waste of time, but I'd gone because I needed the distraction. Gavin had been blowing up my phone for the past week, and I'd vowed not to answer.

So far, I'd been strong. I'd leaned on Cooper and thrown myself into the remodeling work my home needed. It wasn't enough, but it was all I had at the moment. Yet I had a feeling this couldn't go on much longer.

As I walked, I reflected on how this past summer in Boston seemed to go on forever, but now the cool fall air was a welcome reprieve. And the cold temperatures outside matched the icy chill inside my heart.

I sighed, hefting the books higher. One moment things with Gavin were perfect—I'd broken down his walls, or so I thought. And then the next, I was learning from his younger brother, Cooper, that Gavin's ex had died tragically. A little research of my own had turned up the suspicious circumstances of her death.

I needed answers. Part of me wished I didn't, wished I could just move on and forget Gavin Kingsley ever existed. But that wasn't possible. After everything we'd shared the last tumultuous weeks, I couldn't just walk away.

Instead, I'd run to Cooper and demanded an explanation. At first, he tried to play coy—said it was Gavin's story to tell—but I wouldn't let him off that easy. No way. I pressed Cooper until he caved, and since I was fairly certain he had a soft spot in his heart for me, it wasn't all that difficult to get him to spill Gavin's dirty little secret.

God, I'd been so stupid.

My resemblance to his ex was eerie. My long, dark hair fell over my shoulders just like hers, and our eyes were the same piercing shade of blue. We were the same height, same size, and had the same full lips and feisty smile. It seemed like there was only one difference between us—

I was alive.

She'd died in Gavin's apartment. The article I'd read said Gavin had been the one to find her—in the bathtub. The details had been sparse, and a lot of things didn't add up. Initially, foul play had been suspected.

When Cooper had insisted that Gavin would never have harmed her, I hated myself for it, but my mind stewed with doubts. I knew what Cooper didn't—that Gavin had a penchant for rough sex.

Maybe things had gotten out of hand between him and Ashley. I wasn't sure, but that fact had nagged at me, so even though I wanted to move on and forget my affair with the enigmatic multimillionaire Gavin Kingsley ever happened, it just wasn't possible.

I needed to hear his explanation. I wanted to see the look in his eyes while he told me the story in his own words.

Dirty Little Promise 21

After successfully dodging his calls for days, I wasn't yet ready for what was sure to be one of the hardest conversations of my life. So, when my phone rang for the sixth time that day, I'd expected it to show Gavin's name on the display. Instead, it was a number I didn't recognize.

I never should have answered. It had been Alyssa, Gavin's executive assistant, and now he was due at my place in the next fifteen minutes.

I should have been afraid, should have run the other way and fought to erase him from my memory. Instead, I was doing the one thing I knew I shouldn't . . . agreeing to meet with him. Because whenever I was alone with him, I found myself bending to his will more easily than I would have thought.

• • •

Pulling open my front door, I was met with the angry stare of a very sexy man.

A man I hated.

A man I still wanted.

A man who made me feel desperate and confused

and wanton.

Gavin Kingsley's six-foot-three-inch frame filled out a suit better than any man I'd ever seen. And that scowl on his perfectly handsome face? I wanted to slap it right off. Luckily for him, I was raised with better manners than that.

"Come in." I waved him forward coolly, closing the door behind us and leading him into the front room.

He was silent, taking a moment to get his bearings. How strange that Gavin had never been inside my homey little brownstone. Then again, we'd only been dating a matter of weeks. I only felt like I knew him better, probably due in part to our run-ins at the coffee shop over the past year. But I didn't know him, not really.

Gavin's gaze wandered to a midcentury-modern sofa that rested opposite the windows, and the colorful rug in a geometric print that lay beneath our feet. Seeing my home now through his eyes, I felt self-conscious about my little place. If his home was a work of art, mine was a preschool arts-and-crafts project.

His eyes were the most brilliant shade of hazel,

mossy green mixed with caramel brown, and they sliced through me with curiosity every time he appraised me. Now was no different.

What did he think about when he looked at me like that?

All the intimate, stolen moments we'd shared? Or the fact that I looked like his dead girlfriend?

A cool shiver raced over my skin.

"Where do we go from here, Gavin?"

"Pet?" He stumbled over the word.

I'd never heard Gavin so unsure, had never seem him anything less than calm, cool, and collected. This was new. And slightly unsettling.

My confidence rising, I straightened my shoulders and met his gaze. "I'm practically an exact replica of your last . . . submissive? Is that what she was?"

His throat moved as he swallowed, but he made no attempt to answer.

"Oh, excuse me, aside from the fact that she was

younger, thinner, and a *dancer*." I drew a deep inhale through my nose.

What the hell was wrong with me? Suddenly, I was jealous over a dead girl I'd never even met? Yet I couldn't deny those feelings of uncertainty swimming through me. I'd have been jealous of anyone who had Gavin's attention before I did. It was such a wondrous thing, so all-consuming and at times so fleeting.

"Cooper told me everything about . . . Ashley." Her name tasted bitter on my tongue, and I heaved out a sigh.

God, I longed for when I'd been in the dark about everything. Gavin and I had seemed so much closer then, but of course I knew it hadn't been true. Hell, for all I knew, this entire thing was some sick game for him—to seduce the woman who reminded him so much of his ex. And why not?

His gaze slid from mine and a dark look washed over his features. "Cooper doesn't know everything, but let's start with what he told you and go from there."

I nodded and led him toward the sofa. There was no sense in going any further into my home. He wasn't going to be here long.

Gavin lowered his tall frame onto the sofa that suddenly felt miniature, though I'd never noticed it before. He had a way of doing that, of dwarfing everything else around him until nothing else mattered, until nothing else existed but him.

"Let's start with what Cooper told you," he said.

"Right." I folded my hands in my lap. "He told me that you met her at work. She was an escort, and . . ."

I paused, my heart rate picking up speed as I remembered the tender way Cooper had stroked my hair and murmured sweet things when I'd broken down in tears. Taking a deep breath to compose myself, I avoided meeting Gavin's eyes, afraid of what I might see there. I couldn't bear to know how much her loss might still hurt him.

"You dated for two years, exclusively. You begged her to quit Forbidden Desires. Cooper said that she continued entertaining clients there platonically, until you forbade it a couple of months into your relationship."

I looked up, needing some confirmation that this was all true before continuing. Gavin gave me a tight nod.

I couldn't imagine him allowing me to date other men while he and I were together, nor could I imagine wanting to. He was so possessive; it just seemed odd to me.

"There's more to the story. But then, you know that." His voice was rough, gravelly, and I realized he was referring to my love for a good mystery, my passion for stories. "Ashley had some demons in her closet that I worked to keep hidden from the world, and from my brothers. It wasn't their business, but she had a problem with prescription painkillers. She'd started taking them a couple of years before I met her—they were prescribed for an old ballet injury. She had three foot surgeries before finally being forced to retire at just twenty-two. When she watched her friends at the dance company move on, touring the country, getting cast in roles she'd once wanted, she fell even deeper."

None of the articles I'd read online had alluded to any drugs in her system. Something told me perhaps Gavin's influence and deep pockets had kept that part of the story out of the media.

His long, thick fingers reached out to twist the dial on his wristwatch. "She was my submissive, yes. I'm surprised, frankly, that you guessed that much."

"Your dominant nature isn't exactly a secret, Gavin."

He offered me a small smile, the first from either of us today, and I wasn't sure how I felt about it. This was a heavy topic, but each and every one of his smiles was so hard won, I couldn't dismiss it as easily as I wanted to.

"True," he murmured softly, stroking my cheek. "That's true, pet. And you've always accepted me, flaws and all."

"So, why didn't you just tell me the truth?"

A soft inhale and his knitted brow were my only answer. Gavin glanced at his watch. "I'm sorry to cut this short, but I have a plane to catch. Come with me, pet. We'll finish the conversation."

I was fairly certain he'd lost his mind, and my expression betrayed me.

"Don't." His thumb smoothed the line between my brows. "Don't get inside your head like that. Trust me, just once more. You owe us that much."

I swallowed the bitter taste in my mouth, thinking about everything we'd shared. He'd been so open about how he grew up, about his mother being a prostitute, which was no small thing to admit. I thought about our day spent at the arcade, winning tickets and eating pizza. I thought about the way he commanded my body, dominating all my senses.

As much as I hated to admit it, he was right. We weren't done. Not by a long shot.

"I have that charity golf outing in Florida I told you about. You had agreed to come with me . . . before."

I nodded. "Just give me some time. I need to think about this."

He shook his head. "Time is the one thing I don't have, unfortunately. My plane leaves in an hour. I'll be gone for two days. Come with me, pet. We'll discuss everything. I'll answer every question."

The offer was tempting. Just to leave everything

behind for sunshine and palm trees and Gavin's undivided time and attention? The answer would have been a no-brainer a few days ago. I'd even taken the time off work, but now I wasn't so sure.

Gavin rose to his feet, and I followed him to the front door where he paused. "I have to go. Pack your bag. Ben will be by in fifteen minutes to collect you."

I hadn't agreed to go yet, but I felt myself nodding along to his command.

God, it was only noon and I felt like I needed a drink. The effect this man had on me was hard to handle at times. This was no easygoing relationship. It wasn't a harmless crush. In many ways, it felt like life and death—like being with Gavin, choosing Gavin, would be a permanent decision.

He twisted the knob on the front door, then hesitated. "One more thing. When I call you, pick up the fucking phone, Emma. It was torture not knowing if something had happened to you."

Even though I didn't want to agree to a single one of his demands, I nodded. I supposed it was fair—he didn't know if I'd been in a car accident or what.

"Okay," I mumbled weakly.

"This place is great, by the way. Your grandmother would be pleased." And then he was gone, strolling away with purposeful strides toward his shiny black Mercedes, leaving me more confused than ever.

I'd thought a face-to-face conversation would clear things up, but instead my head was spinning. I had no idea what I was going to do when Ben got here, but I only had fifteen minutes to decide.

Gavin had woven me into his web, had integrated himself into my life so completely, and I was held captive. Caught. Unable to walk away—or maybe I was just unwilling.

Chapter Three

Gavin

I stood motionless at the airstrip beside my Mercedes, trying to practice patience and failing miserably. It wasn't a strong suit of mine, never had been and probably never would be. Checking my wristwatch again, I blew out a slow breath. Emma was late.

The aircraft attendant emerged from the hangar, looking annoyed. Despite the cool temperatures, sweat dotted his forehead and upper lip. "Mr. Kingsley, I'm sorry but we need to get moving. We've delayed the takeoff as long as we can."

I nodded. "One more minute. If she doesn't show, we'll go."

He gave me a curt nod and scurried off again.

Where the fuck are they?

I tried calling Ben once more, only to get his voicemail. Again.

Just as I was about to call it and head to the jet, a black limousine turned onto the tarmac, rolling to a stop a few feet from where I stood. Ben hopped out, his expression sheepish as he rushed to open Emma's door.

When she stepped out, I saw nothing but her. The deafening hum of the plane's engine, the sun's bright rays, the stench of jet fuel—all of it ceased to exist. All I could see was five and a half feet of the most mouthwatering curves dressed casually in a pair of skintight jeans and a silk top.

My cock gave a twitch, eager to say hello.

Not now.

Maybe not ever again, but she was here, wasn't she? That had to mean something. But it was the sassy little smirk painted across her pink lips that almost undid me.

"You didn't think I'd show, did you?" Emma lifted her chin as she strode past me toward the jet.

She might have thought she had the upper hand, but little did she know I wasn't letting her go without a fight.

"I'm here for answers, nothing more," she said as she handed her overnight bag to the attendant and navigated the steps carefully in a pair of high-heeled boots.

As she climbed the stairs, I watched her ass sway enticingly and had to remind myself that it wasn't right to imagine what color her tiny panties were. It also wasn't smart to focus on how good it felt just to be around her again.

No, right now, Emma and I were all business until we cleared the air, until things were right again. And if she caught me staring, it would only put her further on the defensive.

With a deep breath, I followed her onto the plane and took a seat in the cushioned chair opposite a table, thinking it best to have something sturdy between us. She followed my lead, sitting opposite me as the crew of three followed us onboard and stowed our belongings.

For a long moment, we said nothing until the attendant approached to ask if we'd like lunch after takeoff. I said yes and suggested she bring a bottle of wine. Maybe that would ease the tension between Emma and me.

Again, Emma said nothing. She merely crossed her arms over her chest and stared as the door closed and everyone took their places, leaving us to the frosty silence.

"Well," I said, clearing my throat.

"You said you were going to talk. So, talk." She motioned to me, her eyebrows raised.

I tilted my head, studying her.

There was a new air about her now. I'd seen her angry, confused, upset, and elated, but never like this. This hard woman was new. Cold. Calculating.

And, unfortunately for me, I oddly found that I liked her almost as much as all the other Emmas I'd met. It took effort to hold back my smile at her domineering tone—like a kitten trying to lead a pride of lions—but I managed, reminding myself again that this was business now, not pleasure.

"I fell for a dangerous man once before, you know," she said. "I'm not going to do that again."

My stomach roiled at the mention of her abusive ex. To be compared to him that way . . .

I let out a hiss and shook my head. Suddenly, any urge I'd had to laugh before was gone. "I'm not a dangerous man. Impulsive, yes. And controlling."

"Demanding," she added.

I nodded. "That too. And jealous. But not dangerous."

She rolled her eyes and let out a snort of disgust. "You? Jealous? Yeah, right. You practically pushed me into your brother's arms."

"And it killed me every time I had to do it," I said, balling my hands into fists at the idea of Emma in my brother's embrace. "But yes, I pushed you to him. It's true."

"It killed you?" Emma's pretty pink lips pulled into a frown.

"Every time you went to him, it was like a piece of my soul was being torn away from me," I confessed, meeting her gaze, hoping she could understand.

But, try as I might, she stayed exactly the same. Hard and focused.

"We're not here to talk about Cooper. We're here to

talk about Ashley. So, tell me about her and don't leave anything out."

"I'll tell you everything," I said. "I promise. But first, I have to know. Did anything happen between you and Cooper?"

"I said—"

"I know what you said. But if I need to focus on telling you everything, then my mind needs to be clear, and that can't happen if I'm wondering whether . . ." I couldn't bring myself to say the words. The thought alone was too much to bear. Of Emma laid out, naked and panting for a man who wasn't me. For my own fucking brother.

"That's your biggest concern right now?" Her tone dripped with disgust, but I forced myself to look her in the eye again.

"Yes. And maybe that makes me a bastard, but there it is." I scrubbed a hand over my jaw and shook my head helplessly. "Emma, Cooper is in love with you, and frankly, he's the better choice for you. I know that. He doesn't have a mountain of skeletons in his closet the way

I do."

"He's my friend," she said, her eyes narrowed.

"He wants to be more than that."

"That may be, but more than that has never happened," she said. "Not really. I already told you everything, and I was truthful. We kissed, and I took a bath in his tub. End of story."

I breathed a sigh of relief, though I wished again for that bottle of wine. I felt like I was in the middle of a hostage negotiation. Now that Cooper was out of the way, Emma and I had to focus on the reason she'd truly agreed to meet with me, and this road was never an easy one for me to go down.

Just as I looked around for the attendant, however, I spotted her rolling the cart down the aisle. "Good, our food."

Emma remained silent as the woman placed two plates in front of us, two glasses, and an uncorked bottle of white wine.

"Enjoy," she said, then rolled the cart away again as I

poured each of us a glass.

"I'm not interested in drinking in the middle of the day." Emma eyed her glass warily, then did the same to mine.

"I find that difficult conversations tend to be a little easier with distractions."

"So, this is going to be a difficult conversation?" She raised her eyebrows.

"For me, at least," I admitted.

We hadn't even begun the conversation, and already Emma was seeing a different side to me, one I didn't show very often. It wasn't easy for me to let my guard down, to show weakness, but Emma always had a way about clawing her way beneath my hard outer shell.

She considered this, then pushed her plate away. "I'm not hungry."

"Don't be stubborn," I said. "You need to eat."

"I don't like ahi tuna salad," she said, glaring at the plate.

"Have you had it before?"

"I don't eat raw fish."

"Right." I cleared my throat. "It's seared, so not totally raw. Try it."

"No." She met my gaze, a gleam of defiance in her eyes.

"Then I'll ask if they can bring you something else," I said between gritted teeth.

"We're ten thousand feet in the air. Where do you think they're going to find something else?"

Letting out a deep breath, I reminded myself to stay calm. "Fine, then we'll land the damn plane and find a Taco Bell."

She pursed her lips. "You wouldn't."

"Try me."

"I'd love to. But I don't eat Taco Bell either. It's gross."

Unable to help myself, I barked out a laugh.

That, as it happened, was the wrong move. She glared at me, snatching her wineglass from the table and taking an angry gulp before facing me down with a warning glare.

"At least let me ask the attendant what else they have."

"Fine," she muttered, taking another sip of her wine.

Folding my cloth napkin, I rose from my seat and ventured to the front of the cabin.

"Is everything okay, sir?"

"Yes, it's fine. But my . . ." My what? Girlfriend? That didn't seem right. Emma had once agreed to be my *person*, but I didn't know if that still stood. "My companion doesn't like the fish. Would you be kind enough to remove her plate and bring her something else?"

"Of course, sir. Right away. We don't have any other entrée options, but we have yogurt and granola, fruit, and some snacks."

"Bring everything you have. She'll select what she

likes."

The attendant nodded and got to work. By the time I slid back into the wide leather seat across from Emma, the attendant was stopping her cart beside us again, offering Emma a variety of choices.

It amused me to watch Emma select a bottle of water and a bright yellow package of peanut candies. When the attendant was gone, Emma tore into the bag and popped a few candies into her mouth.

"Happy now?" she asked as she chewed.

"Yes, pet." I took a bite of my own food, continuing to study her. I didn't comment on the fact that the altitude and sugar would probably make her feel sluggish later. At least she was eating.

"Enough stalling, Gavin. Start talking, or the second we get there, I turn around and go back."

I nodded. "Fine. It's a little hard to know where to start."

"The beginning is usually good," she said, not without a touch of sarcasm.

I took a sip of my wine and gave in. "All right. Ashley was an agency girl, which I know Cooper told you. She came to us just off of her farewell tour with the New York Ballet Company, and she was, well, she was my type. Slender, dark-haired, and graceful. She was slightly curvier than your average ballerina, but knowing you, I'm sure you saw her picture."

Emma stiffened for a moment, then nodded.

"I took her to the Met Gala with me. It was our first date and I thought, well, I assumed a girl like her, so young and having grown up so poor, wouldn't really fit in at a place so fancy, but she quickly proved me wrong. She was the most radiant woman in the room that night, and when she took to the dance floor, she was like no woman I'd ever seen before. She was . . . she was always like that. She fit in every place she went, and she encouraged me to try to do the same thing. At a ballpark, she was one of the loudest people rooting for a team she'd never heard of until she'd gotten to the field. At an opera, she wept for the dying lovers, even though she didn't know what they were saying. She was truly a special girl."

Emma glanced away, but I could see the hurt in her

eyes. I wanted to add that Ashley had a dark side that had eventually stolen her shine. And Emma? She meant the world to me. There was no comparison between them. But I knew any mention of our relationship when she wanted to pretend we no longer had one would only add fuel to the fire, so I remained silent, waiting for Emma to come to terms with what she'd heard so far.

She set her candy down with shaking hands and took a sip of water. Finally, she nodded. "Go on."

"Anyway, Ashley loved life, and the same energy she'd put into dancing she essentially transferred to her relationship with me. She was young too, and it showed. At twenty-two, she was eight years younger than me, but there was something about her that made me not care."

Emma shifted in her seat but remained silent. She refused to meet my gaze but I stared at her, studying her expression the whole time I spoke. The pain, the conflict, the curiosity, I saw it all, and knew the only way to make it better was to press on.

"So, with her youth came a lot of immaturities. She was jealous, even of the women I worked with. She was suspicious of my previous assistant, and absolutely hated Sonja. She was dramatic too. When she was angry, she would make it her personal mission to make sure everyone else was miserable too. Still, she was the breath of fresh air I needed at a time when I was working eighty- to ninety-hour weeks while our business grew. I'd gone on that way nonstop for three years, and when Ashley came around, it felt like a sign. I was thirty and it was time to settle down."

"Were you in love with her?" Emma asked quietly.

I shook my head. "There was a time when I thought I was, but looking back, no. It never got that far, but I did love her. In my own way."

"And you pursued me, why? Because I looked like her?"

I bit the inside of my cheek. I'd dreaded this question, but I knew I had to answer it honestly or Emma would trust nothing else I told her. "Yes, at first. I was intrigued. I have a very specific type that Ashley—and you—fit."

"I see," Emma said softly, leaving me to wonder how

she felt.

"The truth is the first time I saw you, I could hardly breathe—hardly think—hardly move. It's a wonder how I approached the counter and ordered my espresso."

Emma blinked at me, waiting, wanting more. I pushed my plate away and leaned closer to her.

"I battled with myself, wanting you from the very first moment. Holy fuck, did I want you. But after everything I'd been through—the suffocating grief, the condemnation, the fucking media circus—I just couldn't do it again. I didn't know if I'd make it through all that again. And I imagined, maybe you were just like her. Maybe all of my relationships with women were meant to end in death and destruction—like my mother and then my first serious girlfriend. It was better to stay away. But, of course, that was easier said than done."

The flight attendant chose that moment to come back. She removed my plate and refilled my empty wineglass before swishing away again, leaving us alone in the pressure-filled cabin to navigate this shaky new existence.

Emma lifted her eyes to mine, waiting for me to continue.

"But the honest truth is, you and she are two very different people. She was troubled, and difficult at times. Stubborn, immature. But you're independent and strong. Sure of yourself. And also, not. Also seeking. Just like me."

Emma looked down, wringing her hands in her lap. I was laying myself bare, and though I hadn't told her everything yet, I prayed that by giving her all this history, she'd see the real me. Hopefully, she'd see through the fucked-up layers that blanketed my soul, and maybe she'd accept that what happened to Ashley had been an unfortunate accident.

"Then one day I just decided, fuck it. You hadn't found another coffee shop, hadn't changed your routine in all those months, and I was weak, ready to throw caution to the wind. I wanted to see where this could lead. But instead of asking you out, instead of introducing myself and sitting down to talk, I decided to test you. That's what the business card was, you know? A test."

At this, her head snapped up and she held my gaze.

"Did I pass?"

"Beautifully. I never imagined you'd come into the office like that. So brave, my little pet. So . . . everything."

Emma flinched as I leaned forward to touch her, causing me to draw my hand away.

"Are you okay?"

She nodded, but I could see a new sheen in her eyes that hadn't been there before. *Damn it.*

"Emma, look—"

"It's all right. I'm finding that the altitude is making me feel a little unwell." She stood and turned away, hiding her face from me with a sniffle. "I'm going to splash some water on my face, and we can continue this when we get to Florida."

When she was gone, I swirled the wine in my glass wistfully. I'd known no good could come of this conversation. To me, Ashley was all tragedy and heartbreak. The best things about her, the memories of us laughing or joking around, had faded over time. And in truth? I found them just as bitter as the rest of it now.

Still, I didn't want to mar the memory of a good person by sharing too many details of her disease. The way the drugs had taken hold of her; the way she'd lied and cheated toward the end. And the way things had eventually ended.

Still, if not telling might cost me Emma? I had no choice. Hopefully, what I'd shared today had been enough for both of us.

A short time later, Emma rejoined me, her eyes watery but clear.

"Thank you for taking the chance and coming with me," I said sincerely.

She gave me a shaky nod. "What's on the agenda for this trip?"

I released the breath that had been pinned in my chest as I realized she'd been left as raw from our conversation as I had, and had decided to put a pin in it.

"The usual, really." I shrugged. "It's a golf outing with dinner and a cocktail hour. Did you bring along clothes for that kind of thing?"

Dirty Little Promise

She nodded again and then went quiet.

For the rest of the plane ride, there was an Ashley-sized wedge between us that was as tangible as if she were sitting right here. As much as I welcomed the reprieve, there was no doubt.

Eventually, it was all going to come out.

And the only question that remained was whether Emma's feelings for me would survive it.

Chapter Four

Emma

Talk about a bumpy landing.

Not the pilot. He did his job perfectly, lowering the jet so smoothly onto the airstrip, I didn't notice we had landed until I saw palm trees out my window. Gavin and me, on the other hand? Things between us were so rocky, I didn't know if there would ever be smooth sailing again.

We spent most of the limo ride in silence. Gavin had opened up on the jet about his relationship with Ashley, but I still had a lot of questions. I'd been down the abusive-relationship road before, and no matter how much I cared about Gavin, there was no way I would let myself get hurt like that again.

When we arrived at the hotel, the limo driver opened my door, and I was instantly struck by the soft salty smell of the warm beach air. Just being outside felt like a dip in the ocean, and I couldn't wait to clear my head by the water. When I stepped out of the limo, I had to bite my lip to keep from gasping out loud.

This hotel was like something out of a movie.

Since I started seeing Gavin, I thought I was getting used to seeing how the other half lived. But this place? It was unreal, the kind of hotel where celebrities and wealthy politicians stayed.

The doorman greeted us and held the huge swinging door open as we entered the most gorgeous lobby I'd ever seen. Glossy marble floors stretched out in front of us, and a row of gold-tiled columns led us to the front desk. A massive three-tiered floral arrangement stood in the center of the lobby, with more flowers in it than I could count. The backdrop of the lobby featured floor-to-ceiling windows that showcased the pristine beach just a short walk away. I couldn't tell if it was the flowers or the view, but I was starting to feel a little light-headed.

At the front desk, the attendant gave Gavin our room keys, and the bellhop piled our luggage onto a cart. We rode the elevator up sixteen floors before the doors opened with a loud ding. The bellhop led us down a short hallway before pausing briefly in front of our door after he opened it.

"Welcome to your oceanfront suite," the bellhop said, gesturing for us to enter.

Gavin motioned for me to go ahead, his fingertips brushing the small of my back as I passed before quickly pulling back as he caught himself and fisted his hands at his sides. The first room we walked into had a plush white linen sofa on one wall, a flat-screen TV on the other, and a large driftwood-and-glass coffee table in the middle. The wall directly across from us featured floor-to-ceiling windows, giving us the perfect view of miles and miles of clear blue ocean.

I could already tell that it would be hard not to get swept away in the beauty of this place.

After the bellhop dropped our luggage in the doorway, Gavin slipped him a twenty and shut the door behind him.

"Would you like the grand tour?" he asked coolly.

I didn't miss the hint of frustration in his voice, but could tell that he was trying to be civil.

"Why not?" I said, doing my best to hide the excitement in my voice. Even if things between us were icy, I was eager to see what the rest of the suite looked like.

The sleek kitchenette easily put my full-sized kitchen to shame with its white cabinetry, marble countertops, and state-of-the-art appliances. Gavin led me past the breakfast nook, down a small hallway, and into the first bathroom, which had a large standing tub and a sandy-beige tiled shower with a waterfall showerhead. It was all so perfect, I could only imagine how much one night in this suite cost.

And then there were the bedrooms. Thank God there were two.

The first we entered had plush pale blue pillows lining the headboard of the white king-sized bed. A vase of white lilies adorned the bedside table, and a modern light fixture hung over the bed. It was the only decoration, though, because the wall opposite the bed had even more floor-to-ceiling windows, flooding the room with the warmth of natural light. This suite gave a whole new meaning to the term "oceanfront."

"You can have this room," Gavin said, running his fingers over the crisp white comforter. "I assume you'd prefer more time to yourself to think things over." He turned to face me, the sunlight hitting his hazel eyes just right so they were almost glowing.

It took everything in me not to melt right then and there. We could sleep together without *sleeping together*, couldn't we?

When I didn't respond, he ventured a step closer and slipped his arm around my waist.

"Or you could stay with me," he murmured.

His crisp, masculine scent washed over me, and a thousand memories of our time together before flooded through my brain. Tangled sweaty limbs, and murmured filthy words.

No. No, we could not.

I ignored the slight weakness in my knees and shook my head. "I don't think I'm ready to spend the night with you again." Not yet, at least. "I still have so many questions," I said, pulling away from his embrace.

Gavin stepped back, his jaw clenching. "I'm going to get some work done. Dinner's at seven. Until then, I'll leave you with your questions." With that, he quickly left the room.

Dirty Little Promise

I sighed and flopped down on the bed, relishing in how perfectly it formed to my body.

This trip would be a lot harder than I thought.

• • •

At dinner, I decided to ask Gavin my questions after our main course was served. By that point, he'd already have plenty of bourbon and lobster in him, and I hoped that would make him more open to sharing. I could tell my need to know was getting on his nerves. Part of me felt bad to be doubting him this way, but another part of me was frustrated. If he couldn't answer my questions, I might never really trust him again.

I took a sip of my sparkling water, cursing myself for saying no to that glass of wine. Sure, I wanted to keep a clear head for this conversation, but a nice glass of rosé would really take the edge off.

Before I could speak, Gavin cleared his throat, his hazel eyes piercing right through me. "Are you planning on waiting until dessert?"

I narrowed my eyes at him. "No. And I wasn't planning on this being a fight either."

He took in a deep breath and let it out slowly. "I know what I've told you so far has left you unsatisfied."

"I'm not trying to grill you, Gavin, I'm just trying to understand what happened." My voice rose a little at the end as my heart pounded. I was nervous—no, I was scared. So far, he'd told me all about Ashley and their relationship, but nothing about her death.

"I know, pet," he said, holding his hand out in the middle of the table. "Be patient with me."

I stared at his hand for a moment, conscious of the meaning behind the gesture.

He never used that nickname during idle conversation, and I knew he was trying to be reassuring. The gesture was sweet.

Did I trust him yet? Not by a long shot. But there was only one way to let him try to earn it back.

I placed my hand in his and gave it a soft squeeze. Gavin stared deep into my eyes, running his thumb over my knuckles. He squeezed my hand in return before pulling away, then rolled his shoulders back and placed his hands in his lap.

"I'm trying to be patient. So, it sounds like you and Ashley had some similarities in how you were raised." I hoped restarting where we'd left off would get him talking again.

He nodded. "Ashley was a foster kid. She bounced from home to home for most of her childhood, only being adopted later in her teenage years. It wasn't an easy life, but she was tough. Dancing got her through the hard parts. Up-and-coming dancers don't make a lot of money, though, so she came to me at nineteen asking to be an escort. I was reluctant at first because of her age, but she was persistent, and I knew that if we didn't take her in, someone else far more dangerous would."

I thought of Gavin's mother, and the look on his face when he showed me the neighborhood where he grew up. I could see why he became attached to Ashley.

"She was an excellent escort," Gavin said after taking a long sip of his drink. "Intuitive. Her years in foster care made her good at reading people, and she always seemed to know what our clients needed to hear. I guess that's what drew me to her. We were just friends at first. Close friends. But over time, we grew closer. It was like everyone else could see what was happening but us. I became more and more possessive. I was worried about her every time she went out with a client, worried she would get hurt or taken advantage of. It was a mess. I was a mess." He shook his head, running his hands through his hair before continuing.

"After the first time we slept together, I could tell that things with Ashley would be different. I'd found my perfect submissive, and I needed her to be completely mine. I demanded that she leave the company. Between being a dancer and an escort, she was working herself to death. It didn't help that we were all wrong for each other. If the age difference wasn't enough, we both came with baggage, childhood trauma and all that shit. We couldn't see it at the time, but there was no way things between us could have ended well."

He paused, swirling the liquid in his glass and staring at the tablecloth.

"When she got hooked on pills, I knew that something in her life had to change. I grew angrier, more persistent. I told her she needed to find another job, and threatened to fire her if she didn't start looking. But once dancing was out, she was convinced that being an escort was her only option. I thought that pressing her harder would make it easier for her to start looking for another job, to find other ways to maintain her lifestyle. We started fighting more frequently, which only fueled the white-hot sex we often had. We were always on the brink of exploding, and our push-and-pull was . . . intoxicating. Then one day I found her in the bathtub. At first, I thought she'd just passed out from mixing her pills with a little too much wine. But when she wouldn't wake up, I just . . ."

He stopped then and gritted his teeth. From across the table, I could see his jaw clenching and knew we had crossed a line.

"Gavin, I'm . . . I'm so sorry," I said, but he held up a hand to stop me.

He shook his head, staring down at his lap. I'd never seen him look so broken, so vulnerable. The sight of him like this was devastating. I wanted to hold him in my arms, cradle his head in my lap, stroke his hair and soothe him until the ghosts of his past disappeared forever. God, I felt gutted seeing him like this.

Maybe dinner wasn't the best place for this conversation.

Gavin swallowed. "That's it. That's everything. The ugly truth."

"The article I read said there were ligature marks on her wrists and neck. I—I don't understand."

He nodded. "We'd played out a scene earlier that afternoon. She'd wanted me to tie her up, so I did. But those marks had absolutely nothing to do with her death."

"I see," I found myself murmuring.

A few moments later, Gavin settled the bill and led me back to the elevator.

Back at our suite, the view of the ocean matched the darkness of the atmosphere between us. The sun had dipped beneath the horizon only a few minutes ago, leaving the sky a deep and hazy indigo, waiting to settle into blackness.

Gavin stood in the center of the living area, his eyes locked on the quickly darkening horizon and his mouth set in a straight, grim line. Apparently, our talk at dinner had shaken him more than I realized. I'd assumed that his relationship with Ashley was intense, and that was why he never mentioned her. But this man standing in front of me, looking like he was ready for his world to cave in? He didn't look dominant. He looked sad.

I took a seat on the plush white couch and sighed. "Gavin, I . . . thank you for opening up like you did. When Cooper told me about Ashley, I didn't even think about what it must have been like for you to lose her." I thought again about his mother, and how devastating it must be to be unable to protect the women you love.

Gavin responded only by nodding slightly. He had been so vulnerable at dinner. I could feel him starting to shut me out again, like he did sometimes after opening up. It was my turn to share now, and my window of opportunity was closing quickly.

"I wasn't thinking about what it was like for you, because after Cooper told me, the only thing I felt was fear. I didn't know what to do or what to think. I was just so scared."

Gavin looked at me with searching eyes. "Of me?"

I nodded. He walked slowly toward me and sat down at the other end of the couch. He stared contemplatively at his hands for a few moments before looking again at me.

"Were you afraid that I'd hurt you like Nathan did?"

I nodded again, this time turning my face away from him. Tears welled up in the corners of my eyes, and I didn't want him to see them fall. I wasn't ready to weep and throw myself into his arms. I needed to be strong to get through the rest of this conversation.

"What did he do to you?"

Looking up at the ceiling to gather my thoughts, I steeled myself and returned my gaze to Gavin. His hazel eyes were steady and concerned, but not as warm as the tone of his voice made me expect. This felt like business Gavin, determined to get to the bottom of a problem. I could only imagine him going after Nathan, bare-knuckled and ready for a fight after this.

"Nathan was more than controlling," I said, folding my hands in my lap. "He was abusive. He said horrible things to me, called me horrible names. When his yelling escalated to hitting, I was scared I wouldn't leave the relationship alive." I wrapped one arm over the other before continuing. "After he hit me, he'd feel so bad that he'd try to make it up to me with sex, but his kind of loving wasn't warm or tender or gentle. It was brutal and unforgiving, so rough it hardly felt human."

Gavin furrowed his brow. "Rough like how I take you?"

I shook my head. "No, making love with you is different. You like it rough, sure, but you make me feel cherished. I've always felt like you would stop if I asked you to. Nathan wouldn't. He took in a way that was about control, not pleasure. That's all anything was about with him. Controlling me."

For a few minutes we sat in silence, my words hanging in the air between us. I could tell that what I shared worried Gavin. Hell, what I shared worried *me*. Gavin wasn't a violent man like Nathan, but he still valued control. Almost too much. Maybe Gavin wasn't the kind of man to use sex or hit a woman to make her obey, but I worried what other methods he might use.

"Thank you for telling me. It helps me understand things more clearly."

I nodded, surprised by the depth of our sharing tonight, and totally unsure about what came next.

He moved closer, cupping my jaw with his large palm, and I leaned into him, having forgotten how good it felt to be touched by this man. Every time it was electric, and immediately I needed more. Gavin met my eyes, watching me. I didn't move any closer, but I wasn't backing away either.

Lowering his mouth to mine, he pressed a soft kiss against my lips.

"Gavin . . ." My voice broke over his name.

"Missed you so much," he murmured, his lips moving to my throat.

Tugging me closer, Gavin continued kissing me, and my body lit up under his touch. The warmth of his tongue sliding against mine was pure bliss. For a moment, I lost myself in his kisses, in the press of his rather insistent erection against my belly. Rutting against me uselessly, he let out a soft grunt. But I needed more than his grunts.

My first thought was *yes*, yes to everything. To him. To all of it. But then my head cleared and my libido slammed to a halt.

No.

"I'm not ready." I let the words out in a rush, afraid if I let him go further, that would be the end of everything. And this new side of Gavin, so open and bare, was too intoxicating.

"Okay." He stroked my cheek, then stood, smoothing the wrinkles in his shirt. "I'm going to bed. Would you like to join me?"

I stared at his tall, muscular frame for a moment, although I already knew my answer. Even with his shirt still on, I could see the outline of his firm chest muscles, the curve of his bicep under his sleeve. The bulge in his pants.

I shook my head. "I'm still not ready to sleep with you, Gavin."

He nodded and briskly left the room. "Good night, Emma," he muttered over his shoulder before closing his bedroom door behind him.

And just like that, after we'd both shared so much with each other, it felt like we were back to square one. Gavin was cold and distant, and I was left wondering what the hell just happened.

Two weeks ago, I was falling head over heels for a gorgeous man whose dominance and intensity made me weak in the knees. Now, however?

I didn't know if I could ever let him be in control again.

Chapter Five

Gavin

In the morning, I had breakfast delivered to our suite but ended up eating my omelet alone because Emma still hadn't emerged from her room. Last night's conversations were enlightening, and I hoped that now that everything was out in the open, we could put the past behind us and move forward.

Once I'd dressed and gotten ready for the golf tournament, I knocked gently on the door to the adjoining room and waited until I heard her footfalls on the plush carpeting.

Emma opened the door wearing a bathrobe, the creamy swells of her breasts clearly visible, and my cock ached with longing. *Did she sleep naked?*

Before I got the chance to run with that thought, she raised her eyebrows and pasted a thin smile on her lips.

"What's up?"

I cleared my throat and tried to get my galloping pulse under control. Things were still strained, which was to be expected. I would have to take it slow with her if I hoped to have her stick around.

"Good morning. Did you sleep well?"

Her posture softened, and her smile turned more genuine. "Yes. And you?"

"I would have much preferred you in my bed, rather than the company of my hand." I chuckled lightly. "But yes, I slept fine." It wasn't even a question of trying to censor myself. Emma brought out an uninhibited honesty in me. And maybe all that sharing last night had rubbed off on me.

Her cheeks turned slightly pink, and she looked down at her polished toes.

I brought my hand to her cheek, lifting her face to meet my eyes. "Does that make you uncomfortable, pet? To know that I jerked myself last night to thoughts of you?"

She shook her head, but her eyes held a mix of stormy emotions.

Softly stroking her cheek, I leaned in and pressed a kiss to her forehead. "I'm going to fix this." Dropping my hand away, I took a step back. "I have to head to the clubhouse, but I was wondering if I could set you up a spa day while I'm away today. All the works, on me."

She stepped back from the door and grabbed what looked like a beach cover-up from the bed, along with a book and a bottle of sunscreen. Deftly, she let her robe fall open to showcase a blue-and-white polka-dot bikini.

I couldn't tear my eyes away her creamy skin and soft curves.

"Nope, I'm a simple girl with simple plans. Today it's the pool and this book." She thumped the cover of her paperback.

"Okay, well, I'll see you after the tournament, then."

"See you then."

Turning, I closed the door behind me and headed toward the elevator, trying to stop the wry grin that was already threatening my lips. In spite of everything, I liked this girl more with every passing day. What kind of woman was offered a spa day and turned it down to do something that cost nothing?

Emma, that's who.

By this point, she shouldn't have surprised me anymore, but she did. Maybe that was why she drove me so crazy . . . in every sense of the word.

Deep in thought, I made my way to the clubhouse and joined the group of men readying themselves for a long day of golf. It was eight in the morning, but a few guys already had beers in their hands. Typical business-trip behavior. All it made me do, though, was wish I was lounging by the pool with Emma in her tiny polka-dot bikini.

I blew out a sigh and dived into the fray, a smile at the ready. "Good morning, gentlemen. Ready to have your asses handed to you by the master?" I asked with a wink.

As the morning wore on, I schmoozed and passed out my business card, answering questions and pretending to laugh at stupid jokes while my mind was still spinning with thoughts of Emma. Ever since last night, I hadn't been able to get her off my mind.

The things she'd shared with me . . . the things I'd

shared with her. I'd told her things even my own brothers didn't know.

Still, if there was one thing I'd learned, it was that I had to take the next few steps carefully. I would have to be gentle with her, to remember that she'd been hurt in some of the worst ways a person could be.

Inside, my emotions roared at me to kill the man who'd done that to her, but I controlled myself, funneling all my energy into my game once I stepped up to the first tee.

I needed to win Emma back for real, and I was going to. Right when this fucking game was over.

"Mr. Kingsley?"

I turned, expecting to find my caddy ready with a new putter, but instead, the hotel concierge was staring at me with wide eyes and a card in her hand.

"A message for you," she said. "It's urgent."

I took the note and faced the men around me. "Excuse me, gentlemen, this should only be a mo—"

My words died off as my gaze flitted across the words on the paper.

Company crisis.

Call and return to the city ASAP.

My heart skipped a beat and I swallowed hard, trying to maintain my composure. If either of my brothers was hurt, surely they would have told me in the message? This had to be something else, and anything else was manageable. I just had to find out whatever it was and deal with it.

"I'm so sorry, guys," I said, trying to keep my cool. "It looks like I have some pressing business and need to get back to the office. You all have my card if you need anything."

I shook a few hands and then followed the concierge up the hill, past the green, and back toward the sloping lawn that led to the hotel entrance. All the while, my heart was pounding in anticipation as I scrolled through my phone messages, anxious about the news that was apparently too sensitive to text me.

If this was Cooper with more drama, I was going to wring his fucking neck. I had just pulled up a blank screen to tell him so when my phone buzzed in my hand. It was a message from Quinn with a single link, and I paused in my tracks to click on it and wait until it loaded.

A video of a pretty Asian newscaster came to life as I turned up the volume and followed the report.

"Shocking news today as Senate Majority Leader Caster Evans was arrested with several ounces of cocaine while in the company of a professional escort. All signs indicate that both parties were under the influence of the class-one narcotic when they offered the drugs to an undercover police officer at a party in upstate New York. The senator and his party representatives have refused to comment on the events of the evening. The escort, a woman by the name of Stella Malloy—"

A photo of a girl with dead eyes and an otherwise pretty face filled the screen, and I was overtaken by a stab of recognition. That girl had been sitting in our lobby not two weeks ago. Clearing my head, I tried to focus on the newscaster's words again.

"—was also placed in custody and refused to comment. We have reached out to her employers, an escort company by the name of Forbidden Desires, but they have also declined to comment at this time."

The clip ended, and I stared blankly at my phone for a long moment before it buzzed again in my hand. I clicked on the newest link Quinn had sent me.

Again, it was a video. This time a woman with enormous coiffed hair glowered at the camera as she screeched, her nostrils flared. A photo of Stella was embedded on the screen beside her.

"What sort of morality are we allowing into our city? This company—Forbidden Desires—claims that they're an upscale escort service for wealthy men in need of dates, but let's call a spade a spade, huh? This is legalized prostitution right here in Boston, and nobody is doing anything about it. And, if we look at the evidence, who knows what else they could be doing? We don't know where the drugs came from that were in the senator's possession. This Forbidden Desires place could be an underground drug ring, for all we know."

Dirty Little Promise 75

I clicked off the phone and shoved it back in my pocket. I'd seen everything I needed to.

With news like this, we had to get ahead of the story—and fast. Which meant, as the face of the company, I had to get back to Boston and deal with the groundswell of outrage that was probably already threatening to beat down our doors.

In a daze, I made my way to the pool and spotted Emma with oversized movie-star-style sunglasses covering the majority of her face as she read a book with some guy with rippling muscles on the cover. She didn't notice me until I was standing over her, covering her in my shadow.

"What's wrong?" she asked, a concerned frown knitting her brows. "I thought you were going to be golfing all day."

"I was going to, but something's happened. We need to go back to Boston. Right now."

"Is everything okay?" Her eyes went wide and her cheeks paled. "Are your brothers—"

"Everyone is safe and healthy, but there's a business

emergency. We're going up to the room to pack. Let's go."

Without another word of protest, Emma gathered her things and followed me to the suite as I dialed the pilot to inform the jet crew to prep for the flight. When the arrangements were made, I shot a quick message to Quinn to let him know I was on my way, then considered doing the same for Cooper.

Why hadn't he messaged me about this? Avoiding me over Emma was one thing, but this was serious business.

Shaking my head, I shoved my phone back in my pocket and opened the suite door to let Emma inside.

"I'm still mostly packed," she said.

"Me too. The crew should be ready in twenty minutes." I messaged my driver, then called the front desk to pick up our bags.

"Are you hungry?" I asked her. "Do you need anything to eat before we go?"

Emma shook her head. "No. Look, I know you're in the middle of something major, but I just want to know what's happening. I'm scared."

She was pacing in front of the windows, and I felt like shit for making her panic.

"Right." I speared a hand through my hair. "Of course, you would be. I'm sorry. I'm just in crisis mode. Please sit down."

Quickly, I told her about the news story and then about the more colorful media commentary on the event.

"Something like this must have happened before, though, right? I mean, you can't micromanage everyone you hire." Emma frowned and shook her head.

"But we can do thorough background checks," I said. "We never let in girls with drug problems. Not after . . ."

I stopped myself, but the look in Emma's eyes let me know she understood.

"Anyway, we drug test everyone. She must have gotten through the cracks, or else this was a first and she went along to try to fit in."

"It could have been worse," Emma reminded me. "Someone could've died or there could've been a car accident. This is bad, I know. But . . ."

I nodded and stroked her hair, feeling slightly better at her words. "I know. It could have been worse."

My phone buzzed, letting me know our driver was outside just as the bellhop arrived to take our bags. I motioned to them and tipped the guy handsomely before ushering Emma from the room and heading for the elevators again. Already, my head was swimming with a million media tactics, ways to get out in front of this thing and show the world that we were a decent, legitimate business.

"It might just be a matter of letting the news cycle find something else juicer and hoping people forget," Emma offered as the sleek elevator dropped toward the first level.

"Maybe," I said, placing my hand against her spine, but I didn't think so.

A company like ours had always been a risk, but my brothers and I had relied on both the discretion of our clients, and our girls and our books being squeaky clean to prove ourselves. But now that we were out in the public, especially tied to drugs? Wealthy men wouldn't want their names linked with our company.

Emma's voice broke through my thoughts. "You'll figure it out. You always do."

We made our way to the car, readying ourselves for another stress-filled flight. Luckily, Emma seemed to understand. After we boarded the plane and took off, she didn't bother to comment or ask more questions. She merely took out her phone and distracted herself, probably reading stories about the incident to better understand the severity of the situation.

In truth, I should have been doing the same thing. I should have been scouring the Internet, looking for all mentions of the company to see exactly what I was dealing with, but I was in too much shock to bother. The ripple effect of a story like this might dog us for the rest of our days. A black mark this big? We might have to fold if we couldn't scrub it out.

I thought of Alyssa and Sonja, and the rest of the

girls we employed. This was sending all their lives into chaos, not just mine.

But then, as panic started to overtake me, Emma's voice would fill my head again. *"You'll figure it out."*

Offering me a sad smile, she rose from her seat and stood behind me, pressing her fingers to my temples and stroking lightly.

Her faith in me was staggering. Offering her comfort, even though we didn't know quite where we stood yet as a couple? That meant the world to me.

I would figure this out. I wouldn't just cave because things had taken a wrong turn. That's not how this company had been built. There were too many people counting on me.

• • •

When we finally landed, I instructed my driver to take Emma to her brownstone.

She scooted to the edge of the limo seat, then glanced at me, her mouth quirked into a sad half smile. "I really think you're going to get ahead of this. You're brilliant. You just need some time to think. Take as much time as you need, but call me and tell me what's going on, okay?"

I nodded as she stepped from the car and clicked the door shut behind her, leaving me to forge into the heart of downtown and face this thing head-on.

As I expected, a small crowd of busybodies already stood outside the building alongside reporters clamoring desperately for a comment. I ignored them all as I pushed through the rotating glass doors and headed for my floor, knowing Quinn and a task force of publicists would likely be waiting for me upstairs.

Deep in thought, I made my way to my office, ignoring the searching glances of Sonja and Alyssa, and found exactly what I'd been expecting. Quinn was sitting at my desk, talking quickly and quietly with Fiona, the publicist we kept on retainer for these sorts of eventualities.

What I hadn't expected, however, was the man sitting across from Quinn, listening intently to whatever they were saying.

Cooper.

As I closed the door behind me, all three of them turned to look at me. In that instant, I froze and completely shut down for a moment. If someone had asked me my name or why I was there, I probably wouldn't have been able to tell them.

All I knew was that this was the first time in a week I'd seen my little brother—the man who'd told Emma about Ashley. The man who'd tried to ruin everything for me.

And he had the nerve to look me in the eye like nothing had happened?

I saw red. With rage fueling my blood, I launched myself across the room and knocked him from his seat. He scrambled back, scuttling on hands and feet until he pushed himself to stand, and I dove, trying to catch him by the chin and knock him back on his ass. Unfortunately for me, though, we'd been raised on the same tough streets. He ducked, anticipating my move, and aimed a punch of his own at my solar plexus.

I grunted as air whooshed out of me, but in truth, I

barely felt it. My adrenaline was thrumming and I swung again, this time connecting with his nose, sending him reeling back until he slammed into the wall. I approached again but was stopped by what felt like an iron weight on my shoulder.

Quinn had stepped between us, and he glowered from me to Cooper and back again. "What the actual fuck—"

"That fucker told Emma about Ashley," I spat out. "That was my story to tell, and he knows it."

Cooper didn't bother to respond. He merely held his injured nose and glared at me while Quinn rolled his eyes.

"Is this the time? Really?" Quinn shook my shoulder, hard. "Take your seats and put your differences aside. We need to work together on this, and I don't need to deal with your petty bullshit on top of real pressing issues."

The publicist, who'd been standing in the corner and watching everything silently, took her seat again. Quinn made his way back to my desk while I reluctantly took a seat across from him.

His nose still cupped in his hands, Cooper dropped into the seat next to me. "You punch like a girl," he muttered under his breath.

My hands were still shaking as I glared at him, dying to show him exactly how hard I could punch, when Quinn smacked the desk with the heel of his hand.

"Now is not the time for fighting," he said through gritted teeth. "We're going to handle our corporate issues and then, when this clears up, we can sort out whatever you two are fighting about. Until then, shelve it."

He was right. I knew it, and was already starting to feel like an ass for going after Cooper in the office when things were clearly dire.

I glanced at Cooper, who looked back at me, and a silent, grudging understanding passed between us.

"So, how are we going to fix this?" I looked at the flustered-looking publicist and then Quinn.

"From the ground up. We've already lost fifteen clients—"

"Fifteen? Fuck." Cooper groaned.

Quinn glared at him and then continued. "Like I was saying, we've lost fifteen clients, but I think if we divide up the rest and call each of them individually, we have a chance at keeping the majority. We won't issue a statement until later tomorrow, and in the meantime, Fiona is going to distribute a memo to our employees about the incident."

Fiona nodded at this.

"You have the lists for us?" I asked.

"Alyssa is drawing them up right now. And—" Quinn was interrupted by a gentle knock on the door.

Sonja appeared, a pot of coffee and mugs in her hands. The ceramic cups clanked as she set them on the desk between us, and I could feel her lingering gaze searching my face as she glanced from me to each of my brothers in turn.

"It's going to be a long night. I'll order food," she said. "Anything specific?"

"Dinner would be great. We're going to be here for a while. You and Alyssa will be fielding employee phone calls and cancellations," Quinn said.

"Can do, chief. Coming right up." Sonja nodded and stopped behind my chair to press her fingers into my shoulders in an awkward attempt at a massage.

"I'm fine, Sonja. Really," I said.

She nodded, then let herself out of the room just as Alyssa pinged lists to all of our phones complete with client histories and phone numbers.

"Okay, gentlemen, let's get to work," Quinn said.

And so we did.

After everyone had cleared out of my office, I dialed one client at a time, referencing their specific needs and services with every call. Promising them complete discretion. It was grueling, exhausting work, and every time I looked at the clock, it felt as though another two hours had gone by. No politician would answer my call and their secretaries refused to take messages, but others did. There was light at the end of the tunnel.

Fiona's memo was thoughtfully worded, and though a few girls had called in hysterics, the vast majority remained the cool, calm businesswomen I knew they would be. After what felt like seventy hours' work and a half-dozen sandwiches, day turned into night, and I gathered the courage to surf the net for stories about the case.

The senator in question had been released into the care of a rehab facility, but our employee was still in custody. Tomorrow, we'd have to decide whether to find her a lawyer or cut ties with her to save the company. It was a conversation I wasn't looking forward to, but there would be a lot of those as the next few days went on.

When it was finally too late to call clients, I took to the small couch on the far side of my office and hunched over my phone, trying to come up with a speech for what was sure to be tomorrow's media circus.

Before long, my head was spinning. I leaned back on the cushions, desperate for relief from what felt like the world's most pressure-filled couple of days. But then, when everything seemed too overwhelming, I found myself not in my office at all.

Instead, my eyes drifted closed and I was back in the

hotel suite in Florida . . .

• • •

A soft knock sounded at the door. Curious, I went to answer it only to find Emma standing at the door wearing nothing but her tiny blue-and-white polka-dot bikini.

"I think I got sunburned. Will you look?"

She walked past me into the room, stopping the side of the bed, and turned to show me her back and the lush curve of her ass. Just above her bikini bottom was a thin strip of redness, and I swallowed hard.

"Yeah, you're a little burned. But I have aloe in the fridge."

I grabbed the lotion from the mini fridge and returned to her, slathering the cold liquid on my hands. Slowly, I caressed her back, moving my hands in circles as I rubbed the healing lotion onto her skin.

She let out a little moan of relief, and my cock throbbed as I remembered exactly how good and loud and needy that moan of hers could be.

Gently, I slid my hand just below the hem of her bottoms, my fingertips itching to move lower still, to cup her firm ass, to make her whole body slick with aloe and watch her slide against me.

"I know what you want," she said, and though her tone was innocent enough, there was no mistaking her meaning.

I said nothing. I didn't have to.

Instead, I watched as she hooked her arm behind her back and tugged at her bikini top, allowing it to unravel at her touch. When the fabric was nothing but a ball in her hands, she turned to me, revealing the stiff peaks of her nipples, the swell of her creamy pale breasts.

"What are you doing?" My voice was little more than a growl.

"You want to fuck me." She handed me the bikini top. "So, fuck me, big boy. I want to feel you inside me."

Her dark blue eyes dared me to make my move, and that was all the consent I needed. Taking her bikini in hand, I tied her hands over her head and pushed her back onto the bed.

"No touching this time, pet," I said, my voice husky as I sank to my knees in front of her and took her bikini bottoms in my teeth. I needed to see her, all of her. Needed to taste her sweetness on my tongue. But most of all, I needed to feel her.

My cock throbbed as I finally pulled her bottoms to the floor. She dropped her legs open for me, ready and wide, already slick and waiting for me.

With a growl, I moved to lick her long and deep, but suddenly something seemed wrong.

My aching, needy dick was twitching with hunger, but it also felt . . . pleasured, almost sated. But not entirely. I still needed her, needed to feel her warm and wet around me, but it was as if someone had hit the fast-forward button and we were already fucking.

I craned my neck to see Emma's face, but she had vanished from the bed.

Confused, I sat up and opened my bleary eyes.

• • •

My desk. My office.

I blinked again.

I was awake now, but the strange sensation persisted.

I rubbed my eyes and glanced down to find a woman kneeling in front of me, her blond hair covering her face. She stroked my stiff cock with her hand, purring my name in time with the rhythm. Her other hand moved to tuck her hair behind her ear, revealing the last face I expected to see hovering just inches from my erection.

Sonja.

I started to pull away, shock rendering me speechless, but then the door opened and I looked up to find Emma there, a smile of greeting frozen on her face. It was like slow motion as her gaze instantly zeroed in on Sonja's hand on my crotch before the door snapped shut again.

"Emma, wait—" I called out, but I had no idea what to say.

I swatted Sonja's hand away and she recoiled, a ridiculous pout forming on her face. Ignoring her, I sprang from the couch and dashed out of the office, zipping my pants as I ran after Emma.

How could that have happened? Jesus, I'd been dead asleep. That was an assault. Surely, Emma had to understand. Though, in truth, after everything we'd been through, would she even believe me?

It was exactly what it looked like—I just hadn't been a willing participant. How could she know that?

Panting, I finally caught up to her in the lobby, ready to storm past the swarm of reporters into the early morning light.

"Wait! Please, wait!" I shouted and she stumbled to a stop, turning to face me. "Can you just listen?"

"Why the hell would I do that?" Her voice echoed in the empty atrium. "I know what I saw."

"No, you don't. I'm not interested in her. I was dreaming about you, and then I woke up to find her . . . well, you saw."

Emma's eyes narrowed and she stared at me, doubt clouding her beautiful face. "You must have led her on or given her some clue that you—"

"No, I swear to you, I was dead asleep. We'd been up all night." I raked a hand through my hair, desperate now. "Emma, come with me and I'll fire her right now. Even if you don't come, that's what's going to happen. Just give

Dirty Little Promise 93

me a chance to show you."

Her lip trembled and she dashed a hand beneath her tear-filled eyes. "You didn't call me all night. I was worried sick."

"I'm sorry, really. Just, please, for the love of God, Emma, come with me."

She considered for a long moment, then gave me a begrudging nod. Together, we went back onto the elevator and returned upstairs to find Sonja with her arms crossed and her lower lip trembling, standing near Alyssa's desk outside my office.

"What the hell were you thinking?" I blurted, unable to control myself.

Sonja blinked from me to Emma and back again, running her hands self-consciously over her forearms.

Just as she opened her mouth to speak, I held up a hand to stop her. "Get your things. You're fired. Your behavior was completely inappropriate."

Her chin wobbled as her eyes turned watery. "Gavin, please, I—"

"I don't want your excuses. I want you gone."

"I need this job," she pleaded, tears sliding down her cheeks. She looked desperately at Emma as if hoping she would do something, but Emma turned away, struggling to hide her disgust.

"You should have thought about that before," I said, but my voice must have been louder than I realized.

Quinn appeared at his door, frowning. "What the hell is happening?"

"We're letting Sonja go," I said, my tone brusque.

Quinn glanced at Emma and then Sonja before motioning for me. "Gavin, a word. Please."

Gritting my teeth, I followed him into his office and he slammed the door shut behind us.

"What the actual fuck? You're letting Sonja go? She's one of our most valuable—"

"I don't give a fuck."

Quinn turned to face the wall, his hand a fist at his side, then looked at me again. "I don't know what the fuck is happening around here anymore. Ever since Emma showed up, everything has gone to shit. I don't know how she's involved, but I just know she is. Sonja is too valuable—"

Glaring at him, I cut him off. "She could be the queen of England, but I don't care. We're letting her go. She was molesting me in my sleep."

And just like that?

Quinn finally had nothing to say.

Chapter Six

Emma

"Okay, but just give me, like, three sentences, Em. How was Florida? How are things with Gavin? Learn anything new about the situation with the dead ex?"

It was three in the afternoon, and all day, Bethany had been poking her head into my office every hour on the hour, grilling me for information.

I groaned and rubbed my temples before shooting a dirty look her way. "Look, there's nothing to tell. And even if there was, it could wait until after work." I was a bad liar and I knew it, but there was no way I could talk to Bethany about Gavin here. I'd only been gone for a couple of days, but I somehow had at least a week's worth of work to catch up on.

Bethany raised one eyebrow and shook her head. "You're evil, Emma Bell. I don't believe for one second that you and Gavin shared a boring, run-of-the-mill weekend getaway. Those brothers are too sexy and too mysterious for anything they plan to be that vanilla."

She's got me there. "Go away, Bethany. I'll tell you

about it later."

"Fine, but we're getting drinks when you're done. And you're buying. That's what you get for withholding information." Bethany winked and started to close the door before quickly pushing it open and popping her head back in. "Blink twice if you two did the dirty," she said, waggling her eyebrows and suppressing a smile.

"Oh my God, leave!" I laughed as I crumpled up a piece of paper and threw it at her head.

Turning back to my computer, I sighed at all the work I had left to do. My brain wasn't stuck in vacation mode; it was stuck in Gavin mode. And in Gavin mode? It was impossible to get anything done.

A couple of hours later, Bethany and I were walking into our favorite bar around the corner from the library, just in time for happy hour. I got our drinks from the bar while Bethany grabbed us a small table in the corner. As soon as I placed her drink in front of her, Bethany took a long sip, crinkling her nose after she swallowed.

"What's in this?" She coughed, looking at me like I'd just served her cat pee.

"It's supposed to be sangria, but I swear I saw the bartender pour some vodka in there." I laughed, shrugging my shoulders. Bethany said nothing, simply shook her head and swirled the red liquid in her glass.

"It's the drink special of the day, okay?" I said, growing a little defensive. Working for the Kingsley brothers might pay well, but fixing up my beautiful brownstone was quickly eating through that money. If I was paying for our girls' night out, we were drinking the cheap stuff.

"Fine." Bethany shuddered as she took another sip of her drink. When she was done, she drummed her fingers on the table and gave me a mischievous grin. "All right, missy, it's time. Spill."

I took a long swig of my drink, coughing as it went down. Bethany was right. This stuff was *strong*.

"What do you want to know?" I asked, propping my elbows on the table.

"Um, everything?" Bethany said, mirroring me. "Start with what happened when you arrived in Florida."

"Florida was . . . good, mostly. Productive. Things

were tense at first." I thought about our time on the jet. "But during our first dinner, Gavin opened up about what happened with Ashley. Like, really opened up," I said, staring at the red liquid in my glass. "It was the first time I felt like I could really see him. He was so vulnerable . . . almost soft. It was like a glimpse into the darkness he's been carrying around inside him all these years."

When I looked up, Bethany was staring at me with eyes the size of tennis balls. "The powerful, oversexed businessman Gavin Kingsley has a soft side?" She shook her head. "I almost don't believe it."

"He does," I said, swirling my drink.

"What's the catch? Mr. Dark and Mysterious doesn't just bare his soul one day without a catch."

"Well, he shut me out a little bit after that, but I think I understand why now. I don't think he's trying to hurt me when he gets distant. I think he's scared. The only women he's ever loved, he's lost. It's no surprise he's a little skittish when it comes to emotional intimacy."

"He's not the only one with a right to be scared, Em." Bethany's playful smile fell into a frown. "Did he ever explain how his last girlfriend wound up dead in his bathtub?"

I pushed my hair over my shoulder. "Not exactly," I said, weighing what Gavin told me over dinner. "He talked about finding her body in the bathtub, but he got so emotional, I couldn't bring myself to press him for more answers. If you could've seen the look on his face, Beth, you'd know. There's no way he killed her." Especially not after what happened to his mother. I knew now that Gavin was a man who wanted to protect women, not hurt them.

"If you say so." Bethany crossed her arms, studying me. "But are you sure this is the brother you want to end up with? Even if Gavin didn't kill his last girlfriend, it might be nice to be with someone who doesn't have so many skeletons in their closet. From what you've told me, Cooper is like Prince Charming incarnate. Are you sure you don't want that kind of happily-ever-after?"

Staring into my glass, I couldn't help but pause at Bethany calling Cooper Prince Charming. There was no denying that he was a sweetheart, the kind of guy who would cook me a romantic dinner one night and rub my feet while watching Netflix with me the next. But Gavin and me? What we had was intense and as scary as hell, but it felt more real than anything I'd experienced before.

I smiled softly, shaking my head. "After everything that happened with Nathan, I never thought I could trust another man again, let alone allow myself to be in another relationship. Yes, Gavin is dark sometimes, but being with him feels so incredibly different from being with Nathan. Even after everything he's been through, Gavin's not violent or mean. He really cares about me. He's just a little nontraditional in the ways he shows it."

Bethany gave me a sympathetic smile. "Well, if nontraditional makes you happy, I won't be the one to stop you. I just want to make sure you're safe and with the person who will truly take care of you."

"Gavin does," I said, smiling back at her. "Something changed while we were in Florida. I can feel it. Like just the other night, I thought I caught him with another woman, but he explained the whole situation, and I believe him. I could see it in his face. It's like I can read him so much better now."

"Hold on, I'm sorry . . . *what*? You caught him with another woman and you're just telling me this *now*?" Bethany cried out, waving her arms in exasperation.

"That's the thing, Bethany. After he explained what happened, it didn't feel like a big deal anymore. I believe him, I trust him, and that's it. Case closed." I shrugged.

Bethany scoffed, still reeling from this new piece of information. "Who the hell is she?"

"Her name is Sonja. She works for Gavin. Or, worked, I guess. He fired her right in front of me. I feel kind of bad for her, actually. It didn't seem like she had much of a life outside of the company."

"What happened?"

"They had a late night at the office, putting out a media fire. I guess Gavin fell asleep on the couch in his office, and when he woke up, Sonja was on her knees next to him, stroking his . . ." I lowered my voice and raised my eyebrows. "Manhood."

"Oh my God, ew! She's a freaking molester!" Bethany said, loud enough that the couple at the table next to us turned to give us a dirty look.

Dirty Little Promise

Whoops. Maybe the alcohol in these drinks was stronger than we thought.

"I don't know if I'd go so far as to call her a molester," I said. "When I walked in on the two of them like that, she looked at me with the most desperate eyes I've ever seen. It was almost like she was asking me to let her have that moment with him. I think she was lonely and confused. Really confused."

I nodded, trying to convince myself that Bethany was overreacting. Besides, even if Sonja was dangerous, she was out of our lives now, and there was no way Gavin would ever let her back in. That much was obvious.

Bethany sighed, shaking her head. "It's just that, from what you've told me, Gavin sounds like the kind of man who gets what he wants. Nothing more, nothing less. I don't know if Sonja would've done that if she didn't think it was what he wanted."

I stared at her for a moment, surprised by her insinuation. "He fired her on the spot, Bethany. Gavin may be cold sometimes, but he's not cruel. Besides, he would never do that to me. He's a monogamy type of guy."

"I'm not saying that he told her to fondle him in his sleep, but maybe it has something to do with his personality. He has such a dominant, demanding presence, it kind of makes sense that Sonja would do anything to please him. He doesn't seem like the kind of man you want to make angry."

"I didn't realize that was how you felt about him," I said, looking at Bethany with my brow furrowed.

She shook her head. "I just feel like you need to be careful. I know that you care about him, but there's still so much you don't know. When you're leaning toward the cold-and-dominant brother, even though the warm-and-loving one wants you just as much, it makes me worry about the kind of relationship you tend to go for."

I looked away, swallowing the lump in my throat. Bethany was just trying to be a good friend, but her warning totally caught me off guard.

Was I making a huge mistake? Was Cooper actually *exactly* what I needed? My heart said no. But my brain? I really wanted to shut it off with more of this nasty sangria.

Bethany sighed, reaching out to take my hand in hers. "I just want you to be happy, Em. You deserve to be so, so happy, especially after what Nathan did to you. No matter who you choose, I'll be here to support you. Just make sure that whatever you decide, you remember who has the control. Both of these guys are swoon-worthy, sure, but in the end, it's *your* life. You have the control. It's up to you."

I took another sip of my drink, finishing what was left of the now watered-down liquid. My head was spinning a little, but I couldn't tell if it was the alcohol or what Bethany had said to me. Either way, one thing was clear.

I had a decision to make, and I had to make it soon.

Chapter Seven

Emma

By the time Thursday evening rolled around, I'd checked my phone roughly a dozen times and had changed my outfit six—yes, *six*—times. I wasn't sure what was making me so nervous. Gavin had simply invited me to a dinner with his brothers. It was no big deal, really. I'd been around all three of them many times before.

Still, there was something about the curt, gruff tone of his message that had me on edge. He hadn't explained why they were having dinner or why I was suddenly invited, and when I asked, I'd gotten no reply. I'd attributed his crankiness to the most recent outpouring of news stories about the company's alleged sordid dealings, but I couldn't be sure. I had a feeling the lack of sex was getting to him too.

The doorbell rang, and I straightened my top for the thousandth time before heading to the foyer and pulling the door open. I'd settled on a pair of black skinny jeans and a red silk top with gold buttons.

As usual, Gavin stood there looking positively scrumptious while his limo idled in the street behind him.

He was more casual than I'd seen him before, wearing dark-washed jeans and a weathered gray Henley-style shirt with three little buttons at his neck. The scent of crisp, masculine cologne hung in the air around him, ever so subtly, and I wanted to nibble him from head to toe.

"You look stunning," he said, reaching a hand toward me.

My heart gave a little flutter at his words, but there was something stiff and mechanical about the way he spoke. Like he had something else on his mind.

Which he will tell you about as soon as he's ready, a little voice in my head reminded me.

We'd shared a lot lately, and I wasn't about to add to his burden by pressuring him again.

"Thank you," I murmured. "Shall we get going?"

He offered me his arm, and I took it after locking the brownstone behind me. Together, we clambered into the back of the limo as soft music floated through the speakers. It was a chilly night and I hadn't worn a jacket, so I rubbed my arms casually while I studied Gavin's profile.

I could tell he was trying to remain impassive, but it wasn't working. His jaw was locked tight, and the second the car pulled onto the street, he reached for the wine bottle in the chiller and poured himself a glass.

"Would you like one?" he offered.

I shook my head, banishing every one of my inner warnings. "I'm worried about you," I said baldly. "I want to know what's going on. You're acting weird, and you didn't answer my texts."

"Right." Gavin took a sip of his wine and replaced the bottle. "Well, I thought it would be better to tell you all this in person. Things at work have been strained lately."

"I can imagine."

"Sonja leaving was a big blow to the company—"

"That's funny, considering that's exactly what she'd been hoping for," I mumbled under my breath, unable to withhold my anger at the woman.

Gavin just gave me a dead stare and continued.

"Whatever the case, she played an integral role, and we're scrambling a bit without her."

"Are you telling me you're hiring her back?" Anger rose in my chest at the thought, but Gavin gave me a decisive shake of his head.

"No, God, no. It's just that between the Sonja issue and the media storm, we can't be fighting with each other too. I need everyone to get along so we can work together and move forward as a unit."

"Okay." I frowned. "So, something's wrong between you and your brothers? Did I come between you and Cooper again?"

"We had a minor disagreement, but no. That's not it. It's . . ." Gavin stopped and swirled the wine in his glass as I tried to read his expression.

"Quinn doesn't like me? Is that what this is about? I mean, if it's not you and it's not Cooper?"

Hurt and confusion coalesced into a nauseating brew in my stomach. I'd barely spoken to Quinn . . . how could he not like me? And how was I supposed to face him tonight, knowing how he felt? I opened my mouth to ask Gavin why he'd put me in that position without even letting me know until it was too late, but he shook his head again.

"It's not that Quinn doesn't like you. He barely even knows you. He just doesn't like me . . . with you."

Not better. Not even a little, but I nodded slowly, my throat aching with unshed tears. "I see." My chest suddenly felt heavy, and now I saw that I had every right to be nervous about this dinner.

"I just wanted you to be prepared because things have been a little tense."

"But you're hoping once Quinn gets to know me, he'll see what all the fuss is about? Is that it?" I raised my eyebrows.

"Yes, that's exactly it," Gavin said with a wry grin that almost reached his eyes. "I always said you were a fast learner. Now, come on. I don't want to be late."

Looking around, I realized with a start that we'd pulled up alongside a ritzy glass building. Gavin helped me from the car, and a nicely dressed doorman was waiting with the door open as we approached. I smiled and thanked him as Gavin ushered me to the elevator.

With every passing floor, my blood pressure ratcheted up another notch. By the time the doors finally opened directly into the penthouse apartment on the top floor, my knees were shaking.

Almost immediately, my senses were flooded by the smell of rosemary, thyme, and lemon. I took in a deep breath, wanting the homey smell to ease my frazzled nerves.

The place was stunning. Modern, but also masculine and comfortable at the same time. The floors were a striking bamboo in a worn grayish hue that made the place feel welcoming and lived-in, and the furniture was oversized and meant for comfort.

Gavin led me inside and nodded at Cooper, who sat at the dining room table, sipping a glass of red wine. He looked as casual and easygoing as ever, though the skin around his left eye was shaded with a faint purplish color that looked suspiciously like the remnants of a black eye.

"Hi, Cooper." I smiled politely at him.

"Hello, princess." He smiled back, giving me that full-on tilted grin I loved on him.

"What happened?" I pointed to his eye with a frown.

This, apparently, was the exact wrong thing to say. Quinn grimaced at me as he walked into the room in the middle of my sentence, carrying roasted chicken on a platter.

My cheeks flushed as it hit me all at once. Gavin had hit Cooper. A minor disagreement, indeed. I was going to kill him for putting me in this position. If I survived tonight, that is.

Cooper, however, shrugged it off. "Just clumsy, princess. Nothing to worry about. Can I get you some wine?"

I nodded, knowing I'd need something to do with my hands. Clutching the stem of a wineglass seemed just the thing.

Seeing that I was in good hands, seated at the table opposite Cooper, Gavin peeked into the pristine white kitchen through the wide door connecting it to the large dining room where we sat. "Need a hand with anything?

What are we having?" he asked Quinn.

"Roast chicken, mashed potatoes, and carrots. Family-style," Quinn said, emphasis on the word *family*.

So that explained it. This was meant to be one big kiss-and-make-up session. I just hoped that Quinn was willing to accept me and allow me into the fold.

"Perfect," Gavin said, and my stomach rumbled in agreement as he took a seat next to me.

"Can I help with anything?" I offered, but Quinn waved me off as he padded back into the kitchen.

"No, no, I've got it all under control."

I took a sip of the wine Cooper had poured for me, watching as Quinn came out a few seconds later bearing a steaming bowl of butter-glossed mashed potatoes in one hand and a serving dish of perfectly glazed roasted carrots in the other.

"You guys must have been spoiled with Quinn cooking like this while you were growing up," I said.

Quinn joined us at the table, shaking his head. "It

took a long time to develop my culinary skills," he said with a low chuckle. "They're more familiar with Velveeta than camembert, I think."

I smiled. "Well, everything looks wonderful."

Everyone murmured their agreement before we passed trays around, all serving ourselves until our plates were laden with food. Or, in Cooper's case, swimming in gravy.

Together, we dug into dinner, talking as we did. The conversation was stiff and forced at first, but something about the scents of succulent chicken and tender roasted carrots set you at ease. Soon, we were bantering back and forth easily, chatting about work, the library, and current events.

"Did you catch the news last night?" Cooper asked no one in particular, scooping another forkful of gravy-smothered chicken into his mouth. "Talk about a shit show." He shook his head in amusement. "I don't know what's more entertaining, listening to the newscasters fumble through the current events, or scanning the headlines for typos. I'm telling you, the local Boston news is really falling apart."

Gavin took a long sip of his drink and raised a quizzical eyebrow. "You're just pissed because that weather girl turned you down last year when you invited her to the trustees' dinner," he quipped, cocking his head to the side.

Quinn smiled, and I struggled to suppress a snort.

Cooper shot me a goofy grin before nodding in Gavin's direction. "And he's just pissed because the guys on their morning news team are some of our mouthiest clients. Mr. Serenity over here almost popped one of them in the mouth—at their own studio, no less."

"That fucker was threatening us with bad press," Gavin growled. "Whatever he almost got, he fucking deserved."

Quinn rolled his eyes. "Children, please, watch your language. We're at the dinner table. Let's talk about something more stimulating than one of Gavin's unsuccessful attempts to control his temper."

Gavin opened his mouth to protest, but quickly closed it when I placed a hand on his knee. He laid his hand over mine and gave it a gentle squeeze before letting go to take another bite and tell his brothers about the restoration I was doing on my brownstone.

We continued chatting with relative ease, the jazz playlist Quinn put on providing us with the perfect backdrop.

Occasionally, Cooper and Gavin would bicker in jest until Quinn broke them up and made them call a truce, but there was no venom behind it, for which I was grateful. It truly was like a family dinner, and I smiled to myself, wondering what I'd been so nervous about to begin with.

When dinner was over and the plates were cleared away for dessert, I excused myself to head to the powder room only to come back out and find Quinn waiting for me in the darkened hallway. I startled, pressing a hand to my chest, and he held out a hand to steady me.

"I'm sorry, I didn't mean to frighten you," he said, his expression solemn. "I just wanted to talk with you, alone."

I nodded. "Okay, what about?"

"I need a favor," he said simply.

"I'll certainly help you in any way I can," I replied sincerely. He was Gavin's brother, after all. And a good man by all accounts. If there was something I could do to help him, I was in.

"My brothers are both in love with you," he said, his tone matter of fact, as if he hadn't just dropped a bomb on me. My heart clutched in my chest, and I drew a deep, steadying breath. "I need you to choose one of them and let the other one down easy. It's the only way we can all stay together as a family. I know this isn't your fault and none of this was your idea, but . . . well, I've protected them for as long as I can remember, and I would do anything to keep us all together. I'm sure you can understand that."

I nodded, swallowing hard to dislodge the knot of panic in my throat. "Y-you got it." I placed my hand on his muscled forearm, hoping to apologize, to say, well, something, but Quinn took a step back as though my touch had burned him.

Without another word, he turned and headed back to join his brothers, calling out to end yet another argument between them.

For a moment, I stood in the hallway, listening to all of them laugh together, my guilt and shock overwhelming me. I'd never meant to make two men fall in love with me, let alone two brothers.

Could Quinn be right? I knew they both had feelings . . . but *love*?

I straightened my shoulders and took another steadying breath. I'd unpack the huge weight of this later. For now, all that mattered was that Quinn had asked me for something that I could definitely handle. And if this was what it took to keep this family together?

I would do it.

Because, strangely, I was starting to feel like part of this family too.

On shaky legs, I rejoined the guys for coffee cake and half listened to their conversation while I toyed with my food. My brain was churning, and I found myself both mentally and physically exhausted.

At last, things seemed to come to a lull. Quinn sighed, placing his hands on either side of his plate. "Well, it looks like it's time to clear up."

"I'm going to get us all some brandy in the library." Cooper strode off while Quinn started bustling around in the kitchen behind us.

"Let's get some fresh air first, huh?" Gavin asked.

I took his hand, letting him lead me through the sunken living room and out onto the wrought-iron terrace overlooking the city. I wanted to help Quinn clean up, wanted to impress him, but knew the way to do that would be to follow through on the favor he'd asked of me.

From up here, the cool breeze whipped around us, blowing my hair in my face as I smiled at the honking, beeping, and buzzing that was the city on a Thursday night.

"Are you having a good time?" Gavin asked, brushing my hair back from my face.

I nodded. "Very nice. I have to wonder, though." I took a breath and rolled my tongue over my bottom lip, trying to figure out the best way to ask my question. "Is there something going on between you and Cooper? It's not my business, but things seem tense, and I just want to make sure I'm not the cause of it. I know everything has been stressful since the story broke, but—"

Gavin held up a hand to stop me, then stroked my cheek. "Everything is fine, Emma."

He went quiet and I waited, listening to the wind whistle past us. After another long moment ticked by, he finally spoke again.

"Cooper still wants a chance with you."

"I see," I said carefully. "Did you tell him . . ." I couldn't bring myself to say the words. Hell, I didn't even know what words I might have said.

"I didn't tell him anything." Gavin looked me square in the eye, then released my cheek from his grasp. "Emma, I want you to be damn sure that I'm the one you want."

"I am." I breathed out the words, barely thinking, not needing to think because it was all so clear to me in that moment.

He shook his head. "No, you're not. Don't answer yet. Go into the library and let Cooper plead his case, okay? Hear him out, and then decide. Because if you choose me, there's no going back."

There was no point in arguing. I searched Gavin's expression for a long moment, then nodded as I slid open the terrace door and made my way back into the warm living room. Silently, I stalked down the hall to the one room whose door was still open and I crept inside, the wood floorboards creaking underfoot as I closed the door behind me.

As soon as I entered, Cooper turned to look at me, a bemused smile on his face. He nodded to a glass of brandy on the sideboard behind two massive armchairs and I took it, clinking my glass against the one he held aloft.

"So," I said.

Cooper eyed me thoughtfully. "So . . ."

"An eventful couple of days." I let out a deep breath, then sank into one of the leather seats.

"Yes, indeed. But I think we've got a lot of it under control. Just one thing we still need to figure out." His gaze rested on mine for a moment, and I looked away, guilty and uncomfortable.

"When you told me about Ashley, you didn't mention the drugs."

He shrugged. "Gavin has made it clear to me I never should have told you about Ashley at all."

"I'm glad you did," I said quietly.

"I'm glad I did too."

Another long moment stretched between us and I took a sip of the brandy, wincing at the sweet and smoky bite on my tongue.

"Brandy's not for everyone," Cooper said, apparently noticing my expression.

"I guess not."

He let out a deep breath, glancing out the wide windows between the bookshelves before focusing on me again. "Can I ask you something?"

I nodded. "Of course you can."

"It's . . . personal." He reached for the glass in my

hands and set it on the table beside us. "What do you want in a relationship?"

"I'm sorry?" I asked, taken aback by his sudden shift of tone.

"What do you want? Because, the way I see it, I'm looking for someone to give me some of the love I never got. But my brother? He wants to punish women for the love he never had. Our mom fucked us up, and you need to know that you're running into the arms of the most screwed-up one of us all."

I blinked, unsure what to say to that. On one hand, I was outraged that he would speak about Gavin that way. But on the other?

I knew he was right, and I also knew that he would have said exactly the same thing if Gavin were in the room.

I finally settled on, "Cooper, I don't know what to say."

"Say you choose me. We both know I'm the better option for you, that I'm the one who can make you happy and give you the freedom you want and deserve. Do you really think you're going to find that with Gavin?" Cooper's eyes were pleading, even if his voice was not.

He leaned toward me and took my face in his hands. Pulling me up to stand with him and then moving closer still, he closed his lips over mine in a desperate, passionate kiss.

I tasted the brandy on his tongue, felt the rough scratch of the stubble on his jaw, the press of his fingertips at my lower back, and waited . . . waited to feel that spark. The electricity. The hunger.

But I felt nothing.

My blood didn't race. My head didn't swim. My heart didn't pound. And my sex certainly didn't ache.

It was only a kiss, and when it was over, I felt nothing but the lingering guilt of speaking up too late.

He must have seen it in my eyes, because when he backed away, I could already see the hurt. The understanding. The sadness.

"I'm so sorry, Cooper," I whispered. In my heart, I

prayed we could still be friends, but that was probably a long shot.

"I'm sorry too. Now, get out of here, princess. I've got a date with the rest of this bottle of brandy," he murmured with a sad half smile.

Gathering my courage, I stepped out of the room, shaking from head to toe.

It was done. I'd made my choice.

Now all I had to do was live with the consequences.

Chapter Eight

Gavin

I took a deep breath, glancing one more time at the city streets below before stepping back inside the warm expanse of my brother's apartment. Emma and Cooper were nowhere to be seen. Quinn was sitting on the couch, probably waiting for me, a steaming mug of coffee in his hands.

"Want some?" he asked.

I shook my head. "Don't think so."

"How do you think it's going to go?" he asked, and though there was no judgment in his voice, I could tell my answer meant a lot to him.

Scrubbing my hand over my face, I shook my head. "Not well for one of us."

"And you don't know which one of you it will be?"

I glanced away, then met his searching gaze. My fists tensed at my sides, my knuckles turning white. *Have faith, Gavin.*

"Cooper will handle it better than I would have," I

finally admitted, voicing my hopes out loud for the first time to anyone but Emma.

"I think so too," Quinn said, and I knew better than to be offended. He was merely speaking the truth. "The two of you will be discreet while he heals?"

I nodded. "Of course. If it turns out to go my way."

"Good. Then this should all work out fine."

"Just do me a favor and get him rip-roaring drunk when we go," I said, my heart still a little heavy in spite of what I hoped would be my victory.

I hadn't wanted things to happen this way. I'd never wanted to see my brother hurt. After all, when it came to Emma, how could I blame him for loving her? The more I got to know her, the more amazed I was that every man who'd ever met her had managed not to fall head over heels.

"You got it." Quinn took another sip of his coffee as a click sounded down the hall.

Light footsteps announced Emma's arrival. She looked at me, her eyes shining with unshed tears, and I squared my jaw.

"Well?" I asked, not sure what else to say. I could be wrong. She could have chosen Cooper after all.

But the way she looked at me, even with tears in her eyes, wiped every trace of doubt away.

I crossed the room and pulled her to my chest. "Are you okay?"

She nodded, a tear slipping down her cheek. "I just feel so awful. I never wanted to hurt him."

Brushing the tear away with my thumb, I leaned down and pressed my lips to hers just once. "It'll be all right."

I should have felt triumphant, but instead my heart was heavy for my brother's loss.

Emma straightened, taking a step back from me, and turned her attention to Quinn. "I think I better head home. Quinn, thank you so much for having me. Dinner was delicious, and your home is lovely."

"My pleasure." Quinn nodded. "I think I'm going to head to the library for some brandy," he added with a grim smile. He rose from the couch and gave me a reassuring pat on the shoulder before heading past us and down the hall.

I squeezed her shoulders and brought my mouth to hers again. Emma's lush, full lips trembled at my approach.

"Let me get you home," I said.

After I called Ben, we headed back to the elevators and onto the windy city street. All the while, she was silent, her hands clenched into little fists, and I knew better than to press her. Instead, I helped her into the car and held her hand, sitting quietly as the tears slid down her face. Silently, I offered her a tissue and she took it gratefully, dabbing at her eyes before taking a long, shaky breath.

"I hated that," she said.

I nodded. "I know."

"Cooper is a good man, a sweet man. I didn't want to hurt him. I never wanted to—"

"I know you didn't." I slid a little closer and placed

my arm around her shoulders. "Cooper is strong, though. He'll work through this and find someone."

"Yeah." She sniffled. "I know that. I just wish . . ."

"What? That you didn't have to choose?"

She shook her head. "I know I made the right choice. I would pick you a thousand times. I just wish I didn't have to hurt anyone to do it."

Her words buzzed through my body and I held her a little tighter, staring into her eyes as she pressed on.

"But we need to set up ground rules," she told me. "You need to be emotionally honest with me. No more secrets."

My lips tightened into a line, but I gave her a stiff nod. "No more secrets."

"We need to have open, honest communication. At all times."

"Maybe not at *all* times," I joked, but Emma didn't find it funny.

"Always."

I nodded. "I'll try. For you."

I hesitated as she snuggled closer to me, wondering if now was the moment to bring up the one thing that had been on my mind since I'd first met her. The one thing I needed from her in return. I didn't know if tonight was the time to press her, but the weight of this thing inside me demanded to be let out.

"Good. It's settled then." She smiled sadly up at me. "That wasn't so hard, was it?"

I cupped her chin, holding her gaze to mine. "While we're making agreements, there's something else we need to discuss."

She pulled her chin from my grasp. "What?"

"I want to be completely open with you. I want to be myself with you. Which means . . ."

"Tell me, Gavin."

"First is that I told you the absolute truth about Ashley."

She nodded. "I know that. I know you had nothing

to do with her death."

Her faith was everything.

"Is there . . . something else?" she asked, looking at me quizzically.

The need to work through her abuse with her, to make sure she felt secure in our relationship, had been nagging at me—a deep, stirring feeling in my gut the past several weeks. I couldn't put it off any longer, even though I hated to bring up anything that would hurt her.

"Take a deep breath for me," I said.

Emma's brows knitted even further, but she obeyed.

"I need you to know that your past—what he did to you—none of that was your fault."

Surprised at our change in topic, Emma dropped her gaze to her lap. "I know that, Gavin."

"Good, because I need to know that you feel safe with me. It's not just your past I think about. I need to know that as a woman, you feel safe and comfortable with me and our relationship, and the ways I might push you outside your comfort zone."

She looked up, her pretty gaze now dancing on mine. "What do you mean, push me?"

Total honesty, no more secrets.

I couldn't repress my desires any longer. "I need more, pet."

Her gaze stayed locked on mine as the car began to slow. As Ben pulled to a stop in front of her house, we both stilled. It was bad fucking timing. Why couldn't he have circled the block or something?

I could tell that asking for more when she'd barely forgiven me for the Ashley situation was a ballsy move. But, fuck it, life was too short not to go after what you wanted. I'd told her everything there was to know about my past, and now it was up to her to decide whether she'd accept me, all of me. But she'd chosen me tonight, so that had to mean something.

Now was the moment where it all hung in the balance.

Yes or no.

Rather than answering me, Emma reached for the

door handle, opened it, and then slid from her seat.

I stared after her, wondering if I'd blown it, but then she looked at me through the open car door with a shy smile that made my cock pulse with need.

"Are we going to talk about it, or not?"

•••

Emma

Rubbing my hands along my upper arms to fight off the chill, I led Gavin inside my neat little home. Once we'd removed our shoes by the door, he followed me into the family room in the back, and I waved him to the cream-colored sofa.

I flipped on the switch for the gas fireplace in front of the sofa and waited as it flickered before it finally came to life. As much as I longed to replace this with a wood-burning fireplace like was originally in the home, the convenience of it couldn't be beat.

"Are you cold?" Gavin patted the cushion beside him.

"A little." I joined him on the couch, tucking myself

into his side, allowing him to stroke my arms, my hair, warming me and soothing me so sweetly.

"Are you still upset?"

I shook my head. "I feel for Cooper, but I have you now. So . . ." It was hard to feel sad when I was here in Gavin's arms, as terrible as that sounded.

"You do, you know. Have me."

"My person, right?" I smiled up at him.

He leaned down and pressed a tender kiss to my lips. "Of course."

"Dinner was . . . good tonight. Thank you for bringing me."

"I was happy you came. Quinn's an excellent cook."

As much as I loved this softer side of Gavin, and his concern about making sure I felt comfortable with him, I gathered my courage to ask what he meant in the car about needing *more* from me.

I slid back a fraction from his embrace, wanting to be able to see into his eyes while we spoke. "Can we talk about what you mentioned in the car? Tell me what you want."

Gavin's hazel eyes locked on mine, and I had to remember to draw a breath. "I need more, pet."

"More?" I had no idea what kind of *more* he was referring to.

"First, you'll address me as *sir*."

He stroked my cheek with his warm fingertip. His breathing was slow and controlled, his movements deliberate. I sensed a crackling in the air between us.

"More, *sir*?"

"Yes." He stroked my skin again, and I melted into his touch. "More control. More of you. More of everything."

Pleased to see his expression was relaxed, playful even, I ventured another question. "Do you desire dominance and submission? Whips and chains?"

"I think you know that I'm dominant, and that I require your submission."

My brain wandered back to the day in the library where he'd taken me in my office. "Yes, sir." I did know that, intimately.

"But toys aren't really my thing. I don't need more than my body and yours to bring us both to ecstasy, don't you agree?"

I nodded, careful not to ruin this moment. Anytime Gavin opened up to me was a precious gift, one I cherished.

Gavin stroked my hair again, making me feel so precious and cared for. "Thank you for choosing me tonight."

I nodded. "It was always you."

Pressing his lips to mine, he smiled. "That makes me very happy, pet."

"Do you want me to be your submissive?" I recalled the way he'd said that Ashley was his last submissive.

Gavin shook his head. "You're so much more than that."

His words sent warmth straight to my heart. "Is Ashley why you wouldn't let yourself take me how you wanted?"

He nodded. "Not until you knew everything, until you were the one to decide."

The meaning behind his words, his sweet gesture, meant more to me than anything. Gavin craved control, but in this moment, he was giving it to me—I alone held the power to say yes to this, to him. In that moment, I accepted him so fully, it hurt. I ached for him and would have given him anything just then.

Feeling stupid, I asked, "So, um, is there some kind of contract, or . . ."

He chuckled at me, his expression amused. "No, we don't need a contract, Emma."

Maybe that kind of stuff was only in books. But, seriously, how the heck was I supposed to know? Everything about this man and our rocky relationship was new to me.

"I would like to try," I murmured.

"Come."

I rose from the couch, following as he led me to my bedroom. I sensed his entire mood had shifted. Gavin was letting me in—yet again, offering me a piece of himself, and all my senses were humming.

My heart beat wildly in my throat, and my adrenaline soared.

I had no idea what to expect.

I couldn't help but notice Gavin's need for extra control came at a time when things outside the bedroom were more tumultuous than ever—the firing of a key member of his staff, the reputation of his company on the line, the quiet heartbreak we both knew Cooper was suffering. I doubted this was a coincidence, and if Gavin needed to work out his demons on me—I was his.

Entering my bedroom, I turned on the small lamp on my dresser as Gavin's gaze swept around the room. My neatly made bed was dressed simply in white organic-cotton sheets. My bedside table held a huge stack of books, and there was a nearly overflowing laundry basket beside my dresser. There was nothing fancy or elegant about it, but somehow, I knew instinctually that those qualities that made me *me* were what Gavin adored most.

Unsure what to do, I took a deep breath.

"Kneel," he said sternly.

Without hesitation, I lowered my body until my knees made contact with the rug. Gavin's wide stance and his hazel eyes were so sexy as he gazed down on me, and I waited, wondering what might happen next.

Chapter Nine

Gavin

Emma knelt before me, and predictably, that simple act of obedience sent blood rushing to my groin. Her eyes were wide and locked onto mine, and her breathing was shallow, coming in soft little pants as she waited patiently to see what would happen next.

"You're flushed. Are you scared?" I asked softly.

She shook her head. "I want to please you, sir."

I stroked her hair. "That's good." As long as she felt safe and comfortable with me, I'd continue pushing her. "Now, take out my cock."

I wasn't asking. It was a command.

Without hesitation, Emma tugged and released my belt buckle before I shoved my jeans and black boxer briefs down my thighs, exposing my rigid shaft and my balls. I was ready, heavy, and rock hard for her already.

She gripped me tightly in one hand and brought her mouth to my broad tip, treating it to a slow, wet kiss.

I let out a hiss.

Stroking me with both hands, she closed her mouth around me, earning another murmured grunt of satisfaction that came from deep within my chest.

I stroked her hair, gazing down on my pet with adoring eyes. "Mine."

"Yes," she whispered, her mouth full of me. "Yours, *my sir.*"

"Fuck." My murmured curse only spurred her on.

Most girls were timid, shy when it came to sucking cock, but not sweet little Emma Bell. She took all nine inches like a champ, her fist pumping my shaft, the fingers of her other hand lightly stroking my balls. Those were usually ignored, women were afraid to hurt them, and yet Emma handled them perfectly. But she needed to slow down or I was going to lose it faster then I wanted to.

It felt so good, I didn't want to stop her, but I had to. "On your feet," I said, my voice cool and commanding, but my heartbeat was fucking racing.

Emma lifted herself gracefully from the floor and stood before me. She was so petite in her bare feet, barely clearing my chin, and the dominant side of me enjoyed towering over her.

"Strip for me."

Without hesitation, Emma released the little gold buttons between her breasts and drew her red silk top over her head, dropping it beside her feet. Next, she shimmied her hips, pushing her jeans down until she stepped out of them, leaving them in a pile with her discarded top.

She stood before me wearing a black lace bra and a matching thong. Reaching behind herself to unclasp her bra, Emma let it fall to the floor.

I didn't think I'd ever get used to how exquisite she was. Her tits were round and perky, her nipples a pale peach color. She was perfection. I wanted to lick and suck and fuck her breasts, but I maintained my composure.

Tilting her mouth to mine, I pressed a soft kiss to her mouth and ran my fingers along the column of her lovely neck, down over her breasts. When I reached the flat of her belly, I hooked my thumbs into the sides of her panties and drew them down over her hips and legs until they were free. Balling her panties in my fist, I brought them to my nose and inhaled.

She smelled so sweet, making all the synapses in my brain fire at once, reminding me of how good she tasted. But that would have to wait. I needed to be inside her—like yesterday. She was my one weakness, and I was done waiting.

My cock throbbed with need. "On the bed," I said, my voice ragged.

Emma walked across the room and sat on the edge of her neatly made bed. She was following my orders to a tee, and my cock wept in anticipation.

"Lay back, wrists above your head, legs apart," I demanded, and my little pet obeyed like it was her job.

Christ. That did something to me.

I stripped my shirt off over my head and let my jeans drop to the floor. Once I was undressed, I knelt before her parted legs on the mattress.

Emma reached toward me, her fingertips grazing my abs. My cock hung like a heavy pipe between us, but she ignored it for now.

It was strange to realize that the things I appreciated most about her—her femininity, her softness, her supple curves, were the same things she loved about me, the masculinity, the hard planes of my body.

I shook my head. "Keep your hands above your head. Don't make me restrain you."

I was certain she had a pair of nylons in her drawer that would work nicely, but Emma changed course and brought her hands together above her head, which thrust her breasts up and out for my perusal.

"Good girl."

When I grazed her inner thigh in a move meant to tease, Emma quivered beneath my touch. Finding her already wet for me between her legs, I pushed one finger into her snug channel, and she whimpered. As I pressed my thumb against her clit each time I pushed my finger in and out, she let out a broken sob.

I felt her trembling, her pussy tightening around my finger already, and knew she was dangerously close.

Welcome to the club, sweetheart.

"Don't," I warned, my voice a harsh pant. "I want to be inside you when you come." Withdrawing my finger, I leaned down to press a chaste kiss against her swollen little clit.

Emma shuddered beneath me, letting out a groan. "Need you now," she whispered.

Drawing up so I was on my knees before her, I aligned my swollen, needy cock with that beautiful place between her legs. Parting her puffy lips with the head of my cock, I worked myself back and forth over her wet pussy.

In a breathy voice, she asked, "Condom?"

We locked eyes, and for a moment, time stopped.

"I want to feel you," I whispered, my voice uneven.

The look in her eyes confirmed her trust in me. She knew I'd never put her at risk, and she was right about that. I was clean, and I also knew from spying them in her toiletry bag in her suite in Florida that she took birth control pills, so that wasn't an issue either.

For a moment, she didn't say anything, and I

wondered if Emma assumed, rather incorrectly, that I'd slept with the escorts I employed. That wasn't the case. Since I didn't want to get tangled up with a woman who couldn't handle my dark desires, I'd chosen to remain mostly celibate, only straying when my body couldn't take the pressure any longer.

"Yes," she finally whispered.

My mouth attacked hers again in a rush of hungry kisses. Without further invitation, I pressed forward, invading her inch by delicious inch. She was so hot, so perfect, I let out a groan, and she sucked in a ragged breath, taking a moment to accommodate my size.

Resting my forehead against hers, I kissed her parted lips. "So perfect."

"Don't hold back," she whispered.

"You sure?"

Emma bit her lower lip, her front teeth sinking into the plump flesh. "I want it. All of it."

It was all the invitation I needed.

I held her hips, slamming home again and again, not slowing, not showing any mercy. She felt like heaven, and I couldn't even be bothered with the fact that she'd likely have fingertip bruises tomorrow where I gripped her.

Goose bumps peppered her creamy flesh as she murmured, "Don't stop," somehow reading my mind. "There. Right there," she said on a groan.

She was built for me . . .

So wet.

So tight.

So giving.

So *mine*.

Letting me take everything I wanted, and still, she whimpered for more.

With her pulse jumping in her throat, Emma cried out my name.

My jaw flexed. I wanted to memorize this moment. I wanted to devour every jagged breath, every quavering word she whispered. Her cries were like a litany of prayers, and I wanted to grant her each one.

The universe shrank to just this moment—just her and me and the needy sounds of our bodies. I felt unworthy of her trust and devotion, but wanted them all the same.

Emma moaned. "Can I touch you now, sir?"

"Thank you for asking so nicely, but no," I grunted out. "Stay just like you are."

Intoxicated by her, I kissed every inch of skin I could reach, nibbling her delicate collarbone, licking the spot on her neck where her pulse rioted.

Grinding desperately against me now, Emma murmured my name over and over. She was crazed with want, and I fed on her, loving everything about this moment.

She was perfection.

Palming her round ass, I rocked into her harder, taking what was mine. Again. And again.

I wanted to do more than dominate her, wanted so

much more. I wanted to take her to the theatre, to take her to brunch, fuck, I even wanted to meet her parents. Of course, I also wanted to fuck her six ways from Sunday. And my obedient little pet wanted to give me all of that too. Recalling how she'd asked if she'd become my submissive, I inwardly chuckled. No, she was so much more.

Her needy murmurs spurred me on and I pumped harder, lifting her thigh and securing it around my hip so I could press in even deeper.

"Gavin," she cried. "I'm going to come soon."

Taking her bare, feeling her milk my cock, it was everything. I wouldn't last much longer either.

"You don't have to ask, pet." I angled my hips, hitting that blissful place inside her repeatedly in a punishing rhythm. "Get it, baby girl."

That was her undoing. Emma writhed and bucked beneath me, her body tightening around me to the point of pain.

Tilting her face up to mine, I took her lips. "I love watching you come for me, pet."

My cock jerked and without warning, I began to ejaculate—hot and deep within her.

We came together in a hot, sticky rush. My climax was hard and fast, so powerful it made me dizzy. Emma trembled in my arms, crying out my name one last time as I filled her.

Afterward, I moved from the bed and retrieved a warm cloth from the bathroom to clean her of the mess I'd made between her legs. I loved seeing her marked with my ejaculate, but I lovingly wiped away each and every trace from her skin.

Emma rolled onto her side, and I tucked her beneath the blankets, lying down beside her. We didn't speak, but we didn't have to.

This was just the beginning. She'd chosen me, understood my needs.

Now nothing would stop me from making her mine.

Chapter Ten

Emma

The next morning, I woke to find a note on the pillow beside me in Gavin's untidy scrawl.

Had to go. Press conference this morning. Last night was amazing.

— G

It read more like a memo than a love note, but I still clutched it to my chest and rolled over, thinking again of the night before. I'd been unsure at first what exactly he was asking for, but the second we entered my bedroom and his rough voice was commanding me, it was like the whole world melted away and I was all his to mold and shape and please.

And God, had he pleased me.

A little thrill shot down my spine and I shifted in bed, slightly sore, but happier than I'd been in a long time.

Maybe when his conference was over, he'd come back and we could continue where we left off.

Gavin had said he wanted more, but then, so did I. But the thought of telling him what I needed scared the ever-loving crap out of me. How would he react?

I racked my brain, trying to think of a way to tell him of the affections I craved.

Cuddling on the couch? *Yes, please.*

Soft, stolen kisses against my lips and neck? *Always.*

More quiet moments with him at home? *Anytime.*

But I couldn't wrap my head around how I'd approach the topic without sounding like a needy girlfriend.

If there was one thing I knew about Gavin, it was that he needed control. He wouldn't respond to commands in the same way I did, with the obedience and acceptance of a loving partner. This man was broken. He didn't know love. Not in the way that I did, with two loving parents and an easy upbringing. He had never witnessed a healthy, loving adult relationship, and he didn't know how to be in one.

The only way for this to work—for my longings to get through to him—was to show him. *I* had to show him. By example. By brushing soft kisses against his knuckles when we parted, pressing my mouth to his neck while we made love. And I would have to do the scariest thing of all . . . I needed to be the first to say those three little words that terrified me.

I had no idea how he would react, but it was time. Because I did love Gavin, with every ounce of my soul.

Nerves suddenly dancing in my belly at the thought, I ran a hand through my tangled hair and swung my legs over the side of the bed. Rolling to my feet, I grabbed a pair of jeans and a long-sleeved T-shirt, and threw them on before heading downstairs to the kitchen. After making myself a quick cup of tea, I grabbed a bagel and sat at the rickety kitchen table to plan my day.

It was better to keep my hands and my mind occupied. Otherwise, this new, bright relationship with Gavin just might swallow me whole.

The house still needed a ton of work. The moldings

needed to be sanded and the kitchen needed to be painted. It wasn't a day in bed with the world's best lover, but fixing up my home was still something that would give me immense satisfaction once the job was done. I made myself a little shopping list and stuffed it in my pocket before finishing off my tea and hopping to my feet.

Grabbing my purse from where I'd left it on my sofa, I slung it over my shoulder and opened the front door as I took a deep breath of the cool morning air.

At least, that's what I'd intended to do. Instead, I breathed in something rank and unsettling.

Confused, I moved to take my first step, nearly tripping over a mound of wadded-up newspaper on my doormat. It was stained a deep crimson that seemed somehow menacing.

With my heart hammering in my chest, I crouched down and gingerly opened the paper only to slap my hand over my mouth in horror. My fingers trembled as I dared another look. The coppery smell of blood was stronger now, and I held my breath as I stared at the gory flesh that had been wrapped inside. I didn't know quite what I was looking it, but the viscous liquid had soaked into the paper beneath.

My knees quaking, I took a step back and slammed the door. Then, with trembling fingers, I locked it for good measure.

This was no accident. This was a message for me. A message of fury and hatred and ugliness.

Whoever had done this had been here, on my doorstep, in the last few hours. Gavin would never have left if he'd seen the carnage on his way out. That fact alone left me feeling exposed, violated, and the bagel I'd eaten felt like a ball of lead as my stomach pitched.

I wrapped my arms around my waist, trying to settle myself, but if there was one thing I knew, it was that I couldn't be alone.

Not right now.

I pulled my phone from the back pocket of my jeans and dialed the first number in my contact list. The person I knew would protect me no matter what.

"Hello?"

Gavin's deep rumble of a voice sent a wave of calm reassurance over me. I closed my eyes, readying myself to tell him what had happened.

"Hey," I said, but my voice came out as a trembling whisper.

"What's wrong?" he demanded, his immediate concern crackling over the line.

"Is your press conference over?" I asked softly.

"Just ended. What's wrong, Emma?" His voice was more urgent now. There was no downplaying how scared I was, and he could read me all too well.

"I need you to come here," I said, digging up what little strength I had left. The image of the bloody mess was seared into my mind. "S-someone left dead animals on my doorstep. I think it might have been Nathan. You're the first man who's spent the night here since . . ." I could bring myself to finish the rest of the sentence.

"Stay put. Make sure the door is locked, and I'll be right there."

The line went dead, and I shoved the phone in my pocket before leaning against the back of the sofa.

If Nathan had seen Gavin here last night, did that mean he'd been watching me all these months since we'd been apart? That, even when I thought I'd found freedom from my abuser, I'd always been under his thumb?

Tears welled in my eyes and burned down my throat, but I held them back. He'd made me cry so many times before, but I wouldn't give him that power again. Not if I could help it.

Twenty minutes later, my doorbell rang. Although I knew it was Gavin on the other side, I approached the door carefully, looking through the peephole before unlocking the door and opening it.

I was surprised to see Gavin was flanked on either side by his brothers. They all wore grim expressions as they stepped over the gore on the steps.

"We took a look around before we rang the bell," Gavin said, cold fury lighting his eyes.

I nodded, looking from one brother to the next. "Come in." I stepped aside as they filed in like soldiers prepared for battle. "C-can I get you all coffee or—"

"Sit down, princess," Cooper said. "We're going to get you through this."

Quinn gave me a solemn nod. "Let's start with the essentials. Have you eaten? Do you need a glass of water?"

I nodded and then shook my head. "I ate, and no, I don't need anything. I'm just glad you're here."

"Let me make you some tea anyway," Cooper said, making his way into the kitchen.

"I'll go take photos and call the police," Quinn said, more to Gavin than to me.

Gavin ran his hands up and down my arms, doing his best to soothe me. "Are you okay?"

I nodded. "I think so."

The doorbell rang, and when Quinn opened the front door, a man stood there staring down at the mess on my porch. He was graying at the temples but had sharp blue eyes that seemed to take in everything around him. A camera was slung around his neck, and he leaned into the living room with curious eyes.

"Mr. Kingsley?" he asked.

Gavin moved toward him. "Rick, thanks for coming on such short notice."

When I glanced from Gavin to Rick, Gavin introduced us. "Emma, this is Rick Hart. He's the best private investigator in the city. We're going to get to the bottom of this."

Leave it to Gavin to hit the ground running. I hated to admit it, even to myself, but just having him here taking care of things when I was so wrecked made me almost dizzy with relief.

"Nice to meet you, Mr. Hart. Please, sit down."

Rick sat and I joined him, taking the seat across from him as he offered me a reassuring smile. "Gavin filled me in. I'll take some photos, but I wanted to talk to you first. That must have been quite a scare to wake up to."

I nodded but said nothing.

"The police are going to ask you a lot of questions

similar to mine, but because there was no written threat, it's going to take cutting through a lot of red tape to get an investigation under way at all. You understand?"

I nodded again, sick at the thought that this might go nowhere.

Gavin, probably sensing my distress, took a seat beside me and covered my knee with his warm palm. "It's okay, Emma. Rick is going to make sure we figure out who did this so we can protect you."

I glanced at him, slightly encouraged, then turned my attention to the investigator again. "Okay, so your questions?"

"Are you aware of anyone who would want to scare you or cause you harm?"

"Only my ex-boyfriend," I said. "His name is Nathan Jeffries, and he lives just outside the city." I rattled off his address and the investigator jotted it down.

"And why would Mr. Jeffries want to hurt you?"

I pursed my lips and stared at the floor, trying to find the right words. "He was abusive in our relationship. And last night . . . I had a man here for the first time since the breakup."

Rick gave me an understanding nod, then pressed on, peppering me with rapid-fire questions, asking about Nathan's state of mind, if he was unbalanced, if he owned a firearm.

"How long ago did you break up?" Rick asked, his pen poised to write.

"A year ago," I answered.

Rick pursed his lips, no doubt thinking it odd that a whole year had passed and my ex had just now decided to harass me.

And it was odd.

• • •

The questioning seemed to last for hours. When Rick was done, the police came, and I went through it all over again.

The entire time, though, Gavin never left my side while his brothers bustled around my house—checking locks, making coffee, herding people in and out, and making sure I was tended to.

The three of them worked like a pack, my own little wolf pack. A family totally in tune with one another. Not for the first time, I marveled that they had done all of this for me in spite of the fact they hadn't known me very long, and some of that time had already been rocky.

Still, whenever Cooper swooped in with a fresh cup of tea or a sandwich for me, I felt another stab of guilt. It was the first time I'd seen him after our talk. Although he acted as though it had never happened, I couldn't help but wonder if that act was wearing on him. If his true heartbreak was just beneath the surface.

I shoved the thought aside and focused on the questions that seemed to never end.

Hours later, when at last the house was empty of everyone except the Kingsley brothers and me, I made my way into the kitchen and found Cooper standing at my stove, brewing yet another pot of tea.

"Can I talk to you for a minute?" I asked, and he nodded.

"Sure."

"I just wanted to say I appreciate you being here, considering . . ." I sucked in a breath, wringing my hands.

"Nothing to worry about there, princess. You made your choice, and I respect that."

"I just feel so bad for misleading you—"

"Well, don't. Really," Cooper said, and though he'd cut me off, his words weren't harsh. "I could see where your heart was right from our first meeting in Gavin's office. I chose to ignore it because I wanted to believe otherwise. That was my mistake. And I want nothing more than for you and my brother to find happiness."

"Thank you. That means a lot to me." I glanced away, my throat tight with emotion, and took a step closer to rest a hand on his shoulder. "Your princess is still out there, you know."

"Just in another castle far, far away, maybe." He grinned. "But you'll always be my princess."

My stomach twisted at that, leaving me unsure how to feel, when Quinn walked into the kitchen to join us. He glanced at my hand on Cooper's shoulder, and I pulled it away as he spoke.

"Okay, I secured all the windows upstairs and downstairs, and added another lock to the door."

"Thank you," I murmured.

"Anytime." Quinn nodded. "Now, Coop, I think it's time we get back to company business."

Cooper nodded, and the two moved quickly through the living room and back out the front door after saying good-bye to their brother.

When we were alone again, I rejoined Gavin on the couch and nestled close. "How are you doing?"

"Me?" He let out a low exhale. "What about you?"

"I'm better than expected. But I don't want to be alone tonight."

"You won't be," Gavin said.

"Thank you. For everything."

He gave me a stiff nod but said nothing.

"What's wrong?" I asked.

There was a beat of silence and then, "What were you and Cooper talking about?"

"I wanted to thank him. And to apologize for everything."

Gavin grunted his understanding.

"You can't be jealous of your brother, you know."

Gavin raised a brow. "Can't I?"

"You can't. You're the one I . . ." I bit my bottom lip and looked into his eyes. "You're the one I want. I'll admit that I did kiss your brother before, but with him it was just . . . nothing. Sweet, but nothing. He doesn't fill me with passion and need the way you do. When I touch you, I feel a rush of lust."

"Is that so?" Gavin's eyes darkened as he pulled me tighter to his chest.

"It is."

Without another word, I stood and held my hand out to him, ready to take him to my bedroom and spend the rest of my day the way it should have been spent in the first place.

In bed, secure and locked away from all the ugliness that lay in wait just outside my front door.

Chapter Eleven

Gavin

I didn't leave Emma's side all weekend. Together, we read, watched a couple of movies, and worked on our laptops. But mostly, we lay in bed for hours, talking and fucking and doing whatever we damn well pleased. A few times, I even forgot about that fucking mess someone had left on her porch, but by the time Monday morning arrived, it was impossible for me to wipe what had happened from my mind.

It killed me that someone had gotten that close to her and I hadn't been there to stop it. Someone who wanted to do her harm. And now I had to send her back out into the world.

Rage shot through me, and I spent the next ten minutes talking myself down.

I made a pot of coffee and another of tea before Emma joined me downstairs. Her eyes were bleary, but she was dressed in her sexy work clothes, a navy skirt and a peach-colored top that stretched over her cleavage with little silver buttons. Her dark, shiny hair was pulled into a loose bun at the nape of her neck, leaving several dark strands framing her face.

I poured a cup of tea and handed it to her. "I want you to listen to me."

She sighed but took the cup. She knew already what I was going to say—it was the same thing I'd been saying all weekend, but I couldn't go to work without giving this one last try.

"Take the week off," she said in unison with me, and I gave her my best exasperated expression.

"I told you," she said, "I can't do that. I run the library; I don't own it. It doesn't work that way. There's no one to take my place on such short notice, and that makes it impossible for things to run smoothly."

"If this was Nathan, he knows where you work," I reminded her, unable to contain the growl in my voice.

"And he knows it's directly beside the police station. He'd have to be an idiot to try something in a public place that way. Trust me, I'll be fine."

"I'm still going to stay here," I added flatly.

"I wouldn't have it any other way," she replied, taking a sip of her tea as I poured myself a mug of coffee.

I'd tried to talk her into staying at my place instead, but Emma was adamant that she wasn't going to run away in fear. This was her home—it had been in her family for generations.

"I still don't like it," I said.

"You don't have to."

Together, we finished our drinks. When the clock turned to seven thirty, we headed through the front door and shared a quick, hard kiss before I tucked her into the new car waiting for her—complete with the driver I'd hired.

In truth, it was still later than I preferred to leave for the office, but I knew my brothers would understand, given the circumstances. I climbed into the backseat of my own car, closing my eyes as Ben navigated the city streets.

In spite of everything that had happened, I couldn't remember a weekend where I'd felt more in tune with someone. Then again, Emma made that easy. She didn't expect things of me; she just let me be myself. And when it came to the bedroom . . . well, she was a natural.

My jaw twitched as I thought of her again, spread out on her bed and screaming my name while I bucked inside her. Damn, if she wasn't the complete package.

And damn it all if that didn't scare the hell out of me.

"Mr. Kingsley?"

I opened my eyes to find Ben staring at me in the rearview mirror. The car had stopped, and I looked out the window to see the shiny glass facade of the building that belonged to my brothers and me.

"Sorry, must have nodded off."

I thanked him and slipped from the car before making my way to the elevator. Exiting at my floor, I knew it would be hard to keep Emma from my brain and focus on work, but I also knew I needed to give it my best shot.

As I headed through the reception area, Alyssa nodded at me but didn't say good morning. I sighed with appreciation when I walked into my office to find a fresh cup of coffee waiting for me.

Thank God for good assistants.

No sooner had I picked up the mug, however, than my door opened behind me and I spun to find Quinn in my doorway, his face lined with concern.

"Christ, what's wrong now?" I sipped my coffee, pretending the expression on his face didn't rock me to my core.

He shook his head. "I have good news and bad news."

"Which do you want to tell me first?"

"It's the same news. We've been invited to speak on the *Morning Herald*."

"That morning show on the News Network?"

Quinn nodded.

"But they film in DC, don't they?" I asked, and Quinn pursed his lips.

"So, you've spotted the problem."

Frowning, I settled in behind my desk. "Not exactly."

"It's a great opportunity to be heard nationwide. We have to leave right away. You and me. Which means—"

"I'd have to leave Emma alone," I finished for him. "No way. Are you crazy?" I shook my head. "Go by yourself. I can't leave her after—"

"I know, and I get it. But, goddamn it, Gavin, you're the face of the company. If I do all the talking, it looks like we brought in the 'suit' rather than the 'face' of the company, and it makes us look less trustworthy," Quinn said. "It was scary, but Emma wasn't hurt. If there was someone threatening her or she'd been injured, I wouldn't even suggest it. Plus, I'm not saying she should stay home alone. There is another alternative."

"She can't come with us. She won't leave the library," I shot back.

Quinn shook his head. "Not that. Look, I know you're not going to like it, but . . ." He glanced away and cleared his throat. "Cooper can look after her while you're gone. Everything has been ironed out, so there's no reason it has to be awkward, right? We all worked well together on the day of the incident. We can do it again."

I frowned. It was far from the perfect solution, but Quinn was right. The business needed me. Moreover, as jealous as I was of Cooper, there was no one who would take better care of her besides me. It was my only choice right now.

With a sigh, I glanced up at Quinn again. "Have you talked to Coop about this?"

"Only about his running the company while we're gone, but not about Emma. I thought it would be better if the two of you discussed it between yourselves."

"Right. Let me think about it."

"Think quick. They're already prepping the plane for our departure."

I nodded and Quinn slipped from the room, clicking the door shut behind him.

In truth, it felt cruel to ask Cooper for a favor like this. As much as I didn't want to think about it, his feelings for Emma were just as real as mine. And when it came to women, Cooper had never had the layers of brick and cement I put between my heart and the women who shared my bed. He always laid his heart on the table, almost like a dare.

It was something I'd never understood about him. How he could fall in love so hard, so deep, over and over again, and never show the scars of all the times he'd been hurt before?

Gritting my teeth, I wondered if that was what I would have to do with Emma—tear down every bit of armor until she saw everything. Until she had all of me.

Shaking the thought away, I got up from my desk and headed down the hall until I reached my younger brother's office. Gently, I knocked and waited for him to tell me to come in. When he did, I stepped inside, taking a seat before he bothered to offer it to me.

"Quinn already told me about the trip. You have special instructions?" Cooper asked, not looking up.

I shook my head. "No, nothing like that. I wanted to talk to you about Emma."

"What about her?" His gaze snapped up to mine.

"I can't leave her alone after the incident. Not yet." I shifted in my seat and blew out a sigh. "I know this is a big ask, but I was wondering if you could look after her while I'm gone. Make sure nobody hurts her."

Cooper stared at me for a long moment, his gaze searching mine while his lips tightened into a thin line. Slowly, he let out a low hiss and nodded. "Of course I will. Just because she didn't choose me doesn't mean I wouldn't be devastated if anything happened to her. You have my word. I'll look after her."

"Great." I stood to leave, but as I reached the door, I turned around. "And thanks, really."

Cooper offered me a small smile. "Anytime."

As I made my way back to my office, I fished my phone from my pocket and dialed Emma.

"Hello?" She sounded busy, almost frantic.

"Are you okay?" I asked.

"Fine. It's story hour in a few minutes, and someone misplaced the crayons." There was a long pause before she continued. "Is this what you're going to do now? Call me every ten minutes to make sure I'm still okay?" she asked, a smile in her voice.

I chuckled and raked a hand through my hair. "No, no, I have bad news. I have to leave for DC in a few minutes, so I can't spend the night with you. But Cooper is going to come and look after you."

"What do you mean?" Her voice was breathy.

"We got invited to sit with a big news outfit, and we can't decline. But I don't want you alone, so Coop is going to come and make sure you're okay."

"No, no, I'll be okay, really. That seems—"

"Fine," I finished for her. "It seems fine. Cooper had no problem with it."

"I can stay with my friend. She—"

"Can't protect you if someone breaks in. Cooper will stay with you. It's settled, Emma."

She let out a sigh, and silence filled the line. I thought she was going to continue fighting me on it, but she didn't.

"Okay, fine. God save me from you three alpha brothers."

I bowed my head and said a silent prayer of thanks. "Great. I'll call you when I land." I said my good-byes and ended the call so Quinn and I could head to the jet hangar.

As always, I kept an emergency bag in the back of my limo for occasions like these, and Quinn hauled his own down to the car.

"Do you have talking points?" I asked.

"Of course," Quinn said. "We'll go over them on the flight."

While we were in the air for the next two hours, Quinn grilled me on the details of the scandal and on our company policies. But all the while, my head was swimming with thoughts of Emma.

If I had things my way, we'd say *fuck it* and head straight back home. It wasn't that I didn't trust Cooper—I did, even in spite of everything. It was just that I didn't want to trust that she was safe. I wanted to *know* it. I wanted to have her in my arms and never let her go.

Dirty Little Promise   179

Because the truth was, Emma owned me. She meant more to me than my company, more than my own life. And if something were to happen to her?

That was one tragedy I would never, ever recover from.

Chapter Twelve

Emma

Bethany tapped the doorjamb to my office and peeked around the corner. "It's five thirty," she sang.

"I know. Go ahead without me," I said, distracted by my work and glad for it. It had been a long day thinking about everything that had happened, and I didn't know what to expect tonight.

"Huh-uh. I'm not letting you work late with all this freaky shit going down." She crossed her arms over her chest and took another few steps into the room.

I was busy looking over the latest catalog of books for the children's section, but even if I explained what I was doing, I knew Bethany would have none of it. Especially since, truth be told, I was a terrible liar. She and I both knew the order for the kids' section wasn't due for a few weeks. Still, I'd needed something to keep me preoccupied. Something to keep my mind off of what my inevitably awkward night would be like with Cooper.

For a second, I tried to weigh which was worse—the bag of bloody animal parts, or the thought of that heartsick look on Cooper's face. Even now, it was a toss-up.

Bethany leaned over to see what I was looking at, then shut the book on my hand.

"Ouch! God, what's gotten into you?" I pulled my hand away and shook it for effect, although it barely hurt.

"I have a date tonight, and I'm not going to risk getting trapped in this library with you and brutally murdered before I get laid one last time."

As she chuckled at her own awful joke, I blinked and then rolled my eyes. "Thanks for the vote of confidence. Look, whatever happened, it was days ago. Nothing else has happened since. We all need to stop making such a fuss."

That, at least, was what I told myself whenever I snuggled down to sleep at night. And without Gavin beside me, holding me in his strong, protective arms tonight . . .

I suppressed a shiver. We were all being silly. It had probably just been kids playing a prank, or some neighbor mad because I'd taken their preferred parking spot again.

"Emma, come on, what else is going on?" Bethany asked. "You're not yourself, and if it's not the threat, what is it?"

I shook my head. "It's fine."

"Don't lie to me." She jabbed a finger into my chest. "You know that's one of my things."

I nodded with a sigh. "Yeah, yeah. Lying and snakes. Your two least favorite things."

"Exactly." She offered me a coaxing smile, then plopped into the uncomfortable chair across from my desk. "Now, spill. Is it because Gavin is away?"

"How did you—"

"I saw him on the news this morning. He did a good job."

"Good," I said, pushing a pencil across my desk.

I'd secretly watched him myself on my cell, but was glad that Bethany agreed with me. Bethany, who was currently staring at me impatiently.

Knowing there was no way around it, I caved. "Okay, yeah, it has a little to do with him being gone."

"You can stay at my place, you know." She shrugged. "You'd be cutting in on my possible booty call tonight, but for you, I'll make the sacrifice."

I shook my head. "No, it's not that. It's, well, I'm not going to be alone tonight. That's sort of the other issue."

"Okay." She quirked her lips into a confused half smile. "What do you mean?"

"Cooper is staying with me tonight."

"Ah." Bethany gave me a knowing nod and trilled, "Awk-ward."

"Yeah. I mean, we talked about it and he said he understood everything and forgave me, but I still feel, I don't know, weird about being alone with him after everything that happened between us. It's not like he just stopped caring about me. Or me him, for that matter. Just not the way he wanted me to. What if we're eating dinner, and I look up and he's sad or something?"

"Right." Bethany sighed. "Yeah, that sucks. No

arguments here, sister."

"I knew I could always come to you for sage wisdom," I said, offering her a teasing smile.

She shrugged. "What do you want me to say? It does suck. What are you going to do?"

"Pretend I have the flu and confine myself to my bedroom?"

"A good plan." Bethany nodded. "Except, of course, if you had so much as a sniffle, Gavin would come flying back here in a heartbeat."

I laughed. "You're probably right. I guess I just have to be brave and trust that neither of us is going to let this be awkward, and that our friendship is strong enough to weather this."

"And if it isn't, you have my number on speed dial. I'm an excellent third wheel. Ask any of my sisters." Bethany winked, and I laughed.

"Right. Okay, I'll keep my phone close by."

The bell on the door to the library jingled and Bethany bolted from her seat, thudding down the hall until she reached the little lobby area.

From my desk, I could hear her saying, "I'm so sorry, sir, the library is closed for the night. You can, however, use all our online services—"

"No, I'm sorry, I was just looking for Emma. Is she here?"

When the familiar deep voice reached me, my chair scraped the floor as I moved to grab my bag and jacket. "It's okay, Bethany," I called out. "That's Cooper."

I walked down the hall to find Bethany smiling up at him, her neck practically craning to see all the way to his face.

"Are all you Kingsleys so tall?" she asked in awe.

"It's one of our many talents." Cooper grinned, then turned his attention to me. "Hey, are you ready to go? I'm sorry to surprise you like this, but I thought it'd be best if I walked with you to the car."

I nodded. "Sure, but you didn't have to come all this way."

Cooper shrugged. "I'll know for tomorrow. For tonight, I thought we could grab burgers for dinner."

My stomach rumbled at the idea. "Sounds great."

And so far? No awkwardness. Just a good, warm feeling at being around someone I genuinely liked. It was nice, but I willed myself not to get used to it. The night was young.

We said our good-byes to Bethany. When everyone had left the building, I locked up behind us and we made my way to Cooper's car. Unlike Gavin, he hadn't opted for a driver, but slid into the driver's seat of a silver Porsche himself after opening the passenger door for me. I guessed my driver had the night off.

I clicked the door shut and buckled myself in as the car purred to life and classic rock hummed through the speakers. "Are you sure you want to pick up greasy food in a car this nice?"

He laughed. "Life is for living. I'm not going to worry about little stuff like that."

We got carryout from my favorite burger place before making our way back to my brownstone. As we approached, Cooper checked the windows and front door for signs of a break-in, just as Gavin had done in the days prior. Once he was sure all was clear, I unlocked the door and let us both inside.

Without asking, Cooper unpacked the food in the kitchen. He grabbed bottles of water from the fridge, then found plates in the right cabinet on the first try.

"So," he said, setting the plates down on the kitchen table, "I want you to do whatever you would do on a normal night. I'm just here to make sure you're safe, not to be entertained."

"Don't be ridiculous. I'm not going to make you watch *House Hunters*."

"Damn shame. Although, not much point anymore. They always pick house number three anyway," he teased, then picked up his burger and unwrapped it.

I laughed, surprised again by his easy, laid-back demeanor. He seemed so . . . normal. Even if he realized he'd been mistaken about his feelings for me, surely I deserved some anger? But nope. Nada. Cooper just didn't have it in him.

Then again, I should have known better than to think a Kingsley brother would do anything I expected him to do.

With a growing easiness between us, we tucked into our food, and I savored every greasy, comforting bite as ketchup oozed from beneath the bun and onto my fingers. Closing my eyes, I sucked the salt from a fry and ate it like it was the first thing I'd had after months at sea.

"I don't think I've ever seen someone who looks like they love food the way you do," he said with a low laugh.

"I don't think anyone loves food the way I do," I replied with a grin before popping another fry into my mouth.

After we polished off our dinner, we moved to the living room, where I flipped the channels until we found an old classic on TV—*Singin' in the Rain*. It was just at the beginning, and since Cooper hadn't seen it before, I explained to him what he'd missed before grabbing a blanket and snuggling in for the rest. He stayed on his side of the couch and I stayed on mine, but it felt good. Easy.

I smiled to myself, making a mental note to tell

Gavin this when he got home, and then glanced at Cooper again.

Maybe this brotherly thing could actually work after all. In spite of all our history, it could be something good for both of us.

The music over the ending credits drifted into the background as the movie segued into another, and my eyes grew heavy.

"Come on, princess. Slumber party's over. Time for bed."

I jolted upright. *Bed.* God, why hadn't I thought this through? Where was Cooper going to sleep? My guest room held a treadmill instead of a spare bed. And his six-foot-four-inch frame was way too much for my dainty couch.

I stood, turning to face him. "I'm sorry. I can grab you some pillows and blankets, but I—"

He shook his head. "I'll figure it out."

As I readied myself for bed, I tried not to worry. Cooper took one last look around my home, making sure everything was secure before coming to stand in the hallway outside my bedroom.

This was more than a favor. Him sleeping on the floor was the antithesis to the way he should have been treated. But Cooper, being Cooper, wouldn't hear any of it. He tucked me into bed, sitting on the edge of it and patting my back dutifully.

"Good night, princess. Sleep well."

"Night, Coop," I murmured, my eyes already falling closed.

• • •

The next thing I knew, sunlight was shining brightly in my eyes. I stretched, yawning long and deep. Cracking my eyelids open, I spotted Cooper sitting in the armchair in the corner of my room, his large bare feet resting on my floral-pattered ottoman.

His lips curled into a lazy smile as he woke, and he ran a hand through his tousled hair. "Morning," he croaked.

"Good morning," I replied, stunned that he'd slept in

the chair all night.

I glanced around, looking for my phone and finding it on my nightstand. "Shit," I murmured. "I'm so late. My driver is going to be here any minute."

"I'll drive you this morning," he said, rising to his feet and stretching.

I shook my head. "You're already late for work as it is. I don't want to get you into any trouble with your brothers."

Cooper nodded appreciatively. "You're catching on to us."

"Already caught on," I shot back with a wink.

I hurried to the bathroom and took the world's fastest shower, then brushed my teeth before slipping into a pair of black pants and a red cable-knit sweater. Quickly, I shoved my hair into a bun on top of my head and jogged down the steps to find Cooper waiting at the kitchen table with a cup of tea for me.

I snagged the cup and thanked him, taking a long sip and closing my eyes while the warmth poured through my body. "Thank heaven for a good cup of tea."

He nodded.

"Want coffee?" I offered.

He shook his head. "I'll get some at the office. Ready to go?"

I nodded, and together we made our way out the door and down the steps to the street.

"Thanks for, you know, looking after me," I said before Cooper reached his car.

He offered me a warm smile. "Anytime, princess."

I grinned, breathing a sigh of relief as I made my way around his car and slid into backseat of the sleek sedan. My driver mumbled a brief "good morning" before pulling away.

A short time later, we arrived at the library and the car rolled to a stop. I stepped out into the brisk morning air, realizing that I'd forgotten my jacket in my haste to get out the door this morning. I looked both ways, and when I was sure everything was clear, I closed the door behind me and began to cross the street to the library.

Bethany stood waiting for me just outside the entrance, and I waved to get her attention. She waved back and opened her mouth to speak, but I couldn't make out what she was saying over the sudden roar of an engine revving.

Time seemed to slow as I watched Bethany turn from her spot on the curb, her eyes growing wide and frantic. She turned back to me in slow motion, pointing at something behind me.

"Emma!"

But her cry was too late. I turned just in time to see a red vehicle barreling at me, just yards away.

Air whooshed past me as I spun around and bent slightly to launch myself out of the way. Just as my foot left the ground, the metal frame of the car plowed into me, and my body rolled onto the hood of the car like a rag doll.

Tires squealed as the breath left my body, a white-hot pain shooting through my sides. I fell to the asphalt in a heap, the dim sounds of Bethany's screams ringing in my ears. Footfalls rushed toward me, but I didn't move to see where they were coming from. I couldn't.

Because everything went dark.

Chapter Thirteen

Gavin

No matter how many times I went over it in my head, I couldn't say what happened. In my mind, the events of that day were like fragments of broken glass on the floor. I could only see them in a certain light, and when the light was gone? All I could see was darkness and pain.

The fragments I remembered, though, were the ones that still cut deepest.

One moment I was in a meeting with a team of overpriced publicists, who were readying us for yet another press junket, and then the next, my cell phone was ringing in my pocket. On any other day, I might have ignored it, turned off the ringer and gotten back to work.

Not that day. Something in me knew that this was no ordinary call.

What exactly Cooper said when we spoke was beyond me. I couldn't tell you what I said in return, either. All I remembered was my vision blurring and my heart pounding in my throat, and the next thing I knew, I was stepping onto the plane with Quinn while he said words I couldn't comprehend. Not really.

I only knew one thing for certain.

Emma had been hurt.

And I wasn't there to save her, wasn't even there to sit by her hospital bed and ask the nurses about her condition. Wasn't there to make sure she got the best care money could buy.

Damn it all.

Over the course of the flight, Quinn had tried over and over to engage me, but I was too far gone to listen. Instead, my mind was funneling down the old spiral of memories I'd tried for so long to keep at bay. Ashley, too, had gone to the hospital on more than one occasion. First, for surgeries on her feet, and then for stranger maladies that always ended in her taking home a fresh prescription for her beloved pain pills.

Emma wouldn't be like that, I knew, but it didn't change the way my stomach roiled at the thought of stepping inside a hospital again. Or the way I could already smell the antiseptic sterility of the halls clinging to my nose and throat, suffocating me.

Over and over, I relived every visit I'd made with Ashley until the very last one. The one just before the coroners took her away.

"Gavin?" Quinn said, interrupting my morbid thoughts.

We were in the car now, and I looked around to find that we were in front of the emergency entrance to the hospital.

Meeting his gaze at last, I asked, "Did someone send me the room number?"

He nodded. "Yes. And remember, everything is fine. She's in stable condition. Doesn't look like she broke anything. She's bruised and in some pain, that's all. I'm sure the doctors will tell you more, but she should be out of here tonight."

"Good," I said, finally in a place to really let the words seep in. She could have been killed, but the fact that she was in pain and afraid devastated me.

As the sun began to dip low behind the skyscrapers, I

breathed out a sigh. From now on, I would be with Emma—she would never be hurt ever again. I just had to get her better and stick by her side until whatever this was ended.

"I'm going back to the office, but Cooper is there with her now."

A flare of white-hot rage shot through me at the mention of his name, but somehow, I managed to nod. "Right, thanks."

I slipped from the car and rushed inside, checking my texts for her room number. My heartbeat pounding in my ears, I took the elevator to the right floor and found my way to Emma's room with little effort. As I walked, I wondered if I should have brought flowers or balloons or chocolates, anything to show her how sorry I was that I wasn't there when I should have been.

Finally, I stepped inside the private room to find Emma sleeping peacefully. Her eyelids were a little purple and her skin was pale. An IV clung to her arm and I winced, hating every last detail of the image in front of me. Including my brother's presence at her bedside.

"So, you show up now?" I asked him with barely checked fury.

Cooper blinked at me, then frowned. "What the hell is that supposed to mean?"

Another burst of rage bloomed inside my chest. "Let's have a talk in the hallway."

Reluctantly, Cooper got up from his seat and followed me into the near-empty hall. I closed Emma's door behind us, careful to make sure she wouldn't hear any of what I had to say. What I *needed* to get off my chest.

"What the fuck did you do?" I ground out, my voice low but laced with venom.

"Are you under the impression that I'm the one who hit her with my car or something?" Cooper said. "Because—"

"I am *under the impression* that you had one job to do while I was away, and you failed. All you had to do was keep her safe, and here she is, lying in a fucking hospital bed."

He blanched like I'd kicked him, but I didn't give a

fuck. "And what did you want me to do? Stand over her night and day until you got back? Nobody could have guessed—"

"Yes, they could have. We knew someone was out to hurt her. You were careless, and because of that she's here, hurt."

"I didn't know someone was out to hurt her," he said, his pulse throbbing in his throat. "It could've been a prank. I stayed with her last night, and she went to work this morning with the driver you hired for her. How could I have known? And she's going to be all right. She has some bruises and a mild concussion."

"She could have died!"

Cooper raised his eyebrows, then slowly lifted his hands as if to ward off an attack. "You know what, asshole? I took care of her when you couldn't, despite the clusterfuck of feelings I'm still dealing with. Something bad happened and I understand you're upset, but none of it's on me." He shook his head and stared at his feet, cupping one hand to the back of his neck. "I've had enough. I can't deal with this anymore. You and Emma can have each other. I'm done."

Without another word, he turned on his heel and headed to the elevator. I should have gone after him, but I didn't have time to worry about that now. In fact, I was certain I'd be better off if I didn't have to see his reckless, stupid face for a few days.

Right now, all that mattered was Emma, and I wasn't going to waste another moment before seeing her again. Slowly, I opened the door to her room again to find her squinting up at the television, a massive remote in her small hands.

"They don't have any good channels at hospitals," she said, though she grinned weakly at me as she spoke.

"Pet," I murmured, my heart clenching at the paleness of her cheeks. "How are you feeling?"

She shrugged. "I've been better. How was your trip?"

"Does that matter?" I took the seat beside her bed and reached for her hand after brushing the remote away.

"Sure, it does. I like hearing about your exciting life. Beats the hell out of my boring one."

"Yeah, your life really does look pretty boring right

about now."

She rolled her eyes, and I could tell she was trying not to look at me. "Where did Cooper go?"

"He had to leave. I told him you were in good hands, though."

"Whose?" she teased, and I kissed her cheek.

"Don't make fun of me. It's been a stressful day."

"I'm so sorry for your struggle. You're right; the girl in the hospital should be more sensitive," she joked, clearly trying to make me feel better.

"You're damn right. Besides, you won't be in here much longer. Word on the street is they're letting you out soon."

"That's a shame," she said with a shrug. "I don't have nearly as many Jell-O cups at my house."

"I'll get you all the Jell-O cups you want."

And I did. The second we left the hospital a few hours later, I texted Ben, asking him to go to the store and pick up everything Emma could possibly need. Jell-O and pudding, fixings for sandwiches, a dozen different boxes of tea. Anything I thought she might like.

"I have bruises and a headache that's almost gone, not a terminal disease. You don't have to baby me," she said as he delivered the items to her front door.

I scoffed. "Oh, I'm babying you. You just have to get used to it."

Did she not know me at all? I wasn't about to let her go through this alone.

Instead, I fetched everything she would want or need before she even asked for it. I called in to her work for her and held her while she slept—and while she dreamed. When she cried out, I was there to calm her back to sleep.

Emma could pretend to be tough if she wanted to, but there was no question she was afraid. The police still had no leads, either on the hit-and-run or the bloody mess left at her door, and her nerves and mine were starting to fray.

• • •

After a few days, I was sure my hovering was starting to annoy her, but most of the time, I thought she found it endearing. Which was good. All I needed her to know was that I was going to take care of her.

Always, if she'd let me.

"I'm going to get bed sores if you don't let me start doing things myself," she said on the fourth day of my doting on her.

She probably had a point. I hadn't let her out of my sight.

"Baby, you'd still look cute with bed sores."

She rolled her eyes. "Are you going to let me take a bath on my own, or—"

"I'm going to carry you up the stairs and put you in the bath," I said.

"Of course you are," she mumbled, her tone sarcastic.

Not wanting to listen to the rest of her protests, I went upstairs and drew her bath, making sure there were plenty of bath salts and bubbles, before heading downstairs and scooping her into my arms. By this point, she knew better than to argue, and when we reached the bathroom and she stripped down to nothing, I helped her into the tub and lathered a loofah while she breathed in the lavender bath oil.

"Let me do that. You go downstairs and take a break. I'll call for you when I need help getting out."

"Emma—"

"Gavin," she said. "Really. Trust me to do this one thing myself. I'm giving myself two days to sulk and be afraid, and then I'm going back to work and getting on with my life. So, I've got to start somewhere."

Only the certainty of her tone made me hand over the loofah to her outstretched hand.

"You promise you'll call when you need help getting out?"

"Fine," she said. "Now, go relax for a while."

I straightened the sheets on Emma's bed, but no sooner had I finished fluffing her pillows than the doorbell rang.

I frowned and headed down the stairs. In all the days I'd been here, only Bethany had come to visit. For all I knew, this could have been Emma's attempted murderer, coming to make sure the job got done right this time.

As I strode toward the door with my fists clenched, I almost hoped for it. I was fairly certain I could kill the motherfucker with my bare hands.

I peeked through the peephole and then twisted the knob to find both my brothers waiting for me on the stoop.

"What's wrong? I'm off work for the week, I told you," I said as they stepped past me into the foyer.

"We know," Quinn said. "But you also haven't been answering your phone, and we need to talk to you."

This, strictly speaking, wasn't true. I'd been answering my phone . . . for everyone but my brothers. I just didn't want to deal with work yet, not until I was sure Emma was safe and better.

"Okay," I said. "What's going on?"

"I'm leaving," Cooper said bluntly.

I blinked, my mind reeling. "The company?"

"The state. I need some space, and I think this is the best move for all of us. I'm going to open a new branch of the business in a new city and get myself a fresh start." His gaze was shuttered, and my gut churned at his icy expression.

I turned my attention to Quinn. "And what do you have to say about this?"

"I'm torn. This family feels broken now, and things don't seem to be getting better. But from a business perspective, it would be the right time to purchase new real estate."

I nodded and glanced at Cooper. "When will you go?"

"When we know for sure that Emma is all right and out of danger, I guess. For now, I'm trying to figure that out."

I knew I should argue, maybe even apologize for blaming him. But it was all too raw, and I couldn't seem to push the words past my throat. "Right."

"Gavin . . ."

Emma's voice echoed down the stairs, and my brothers looked at me with understanding, sad eyes.

"Well, you're needed here. We'll discuss more details when you're back," Quinn said.

"Okay."

Cooper said nothing. Instead, he turned and headed back down the steps with Quinn trailing behind him.

When they were gone, I locked the door and called back to Emma, "Coming," as I trekked up the stairs. I reached the bathroom and she glanced at me, but as soon as her gaze met mine, the soft smile on her lips died away.

"What's wrong? Who was at the door?"

"Nothing's wrong," I assured her with a fixed smile. "It was the guys. Just some business stuff, but it's nothing that we need to worry about. I'm only thinking about you right now. Tell me what you need, pet."

Her blue eyes darkened as she looked me up and down. "I need you to join me."

"In the tub?" I laughed. "No way."

"Then out of the tub. On the floor. On the counter." She looked me over again, a slightly desperate edge to her chuckle. "Anywhere. I don't want to feel like an invalid anymore. I want to touch you and—"

I bit back a groan as my cock instantly swelled at the thought. It had been almost a week since we'd touched like that, and I could still feel the heat of her around me.

I shoved back the thought and shook my head. "You're in no state for something like that."

She pouted, lifting a hand toward me. "Gavin, please? I need you."

Her voice was so raw with need that my cock grew thick and achy, but I forced myself to remain strong.

"Not until you're better."

"Fine, then. Can you help me dry off, at least?"

She rose a brow in challenge, but I ignored it as I rolled up my sleeves and lifted her from the tub. Once she was standing on her feet again, I handed her a towel, but she shook her head.

"I want you to do it."

"Emma . . ."

"What? I thought you wanted to do everything for me. Please?"

When she raised her eyebrows, I let out an exasperated sigh. She was determined to get her way, and it was beyond me to not let her have it. I would have given her anything just then—she was dewy and pink from the heat of her bath.

Bending low, I brushed the towel along her ankles and feet, then higher, up her creamy thighs. As I wiped the droplets from her skin, she spread her legs a fraction for me, offering me a better view of her, and I clenched my jaw as I moved to the next leg.

"I know what you're doing," I said, my chest tight.

"Getting dry?" she said in her most innocent voice.

I sucked in a steadying breath and grunted. "Don't toy with me."

"I would never." Her lips twitched with a smirk.

"Emma, I don't want to hurt you. Your ribs . . ." But then I was moving up to her stomach, sliding the towel over the white plane of her skin and watching as her nipples stiffened at my touch.

I swallowed hard, then moved to dry her perfect, round breasts. It took all my internal fortitude not to stop right then and drop my mouth to those silky pink tips and suck them hard so I could feel them grow stiff in my mouth.

"I want you," she whispered. "And I can see you want me too."

"You're not in shape to be jostled around like that, Emma."

"Then let's not do that. We can do other things." She moved to get on her knees, but I held out a hand to stop her.

"No. No fucking way. If we're doing this, then tonight is about you."

Slowly, I interlaced her fingers with mine and led her

into the bedroom.

"Lay on the edge of the bed and spread your legs for me," I demanded, suddenly desperate to feel her clit against my tongue.

"But, Gavin, I want to be with you."

"You will be. And don't argue," I said.

Silently, she did as she was told and lay back, allowing me to see every inch of her milky-white skin and the pretty pink space between her thighs.

Staring at her, I tugged my own clothes away, not caring where they fell. She watched me, her pupils dilated as I pulled my boxers down and allowed my length to spring forward. Tempting me, she licked her lips at the sight, and I gripped my shaft, stroking it to quell the insistent ache that always came when I saw her bare.

Working myself up and down, I got to my knees in front of her and licked her in soft strokes, teasing her until I was ready to explore the space where I knew she needed me most.

She let out a gentle moan and I growled low in my

throat, praising her for the sound even as I worked my cock in longer strokes, desperate for more.

"That's it, baby. Show me how much you like it," I whispered, then lowered my mouth to her again, lapping her core until I finally reached the tight bundle of nerves that I knew was begging for my attention.

Slowly, I circled her, loving the little twitch of her hips as she responded to my touch.

"Gavin," she moaned. "You're so good at this."

"Yes, beautiful. Just like that," I told her. And she did. With every push and pull of my tongue, she rocked her hips into me, pushing me to kiss her deeper, suck her harder, to work her to the breaking point.

As she moved, I gripped my shaft tighter, closing my eyes as I imagined her rocking into me this way, pulling my cock deeper into her body with every little spasm.

God, I couldn't wait to be with her again, but for tonight, this would have to be enough. And with the taste of her on my tongue? I wasn't about to complain.

"I need you," she whimpered, and I licked her long

and deep again before pushing two fingers into her waiting heat, moving in and out as she continued to roll her hips. "Fuck me, Gavin."

She was close—I could feel it in the tightness of her walls, the neediness of her thrusts. She moved faster now and I gripped my cock even harder, working myself in long strokes.

She lifted to her elbows, her gaze drawn to my mouth, then to where my hand fisted my shaft.

"So hot, watching you touch yourself," she murmured, her gaze soft and pleading. "Are you going to make yourself come?"

"After you," I said, my tongue lapping at her in lazy circles.

I bit down on her inner thigh in a soft nibble, still fucking her with my fingers. When I brought my lips to her sensitive bundle and sucked—hard—her body pulsed and shook, clutching my fingers.

This was the moment. She let out a low, deep moan and I closed my eyes, savoring the greed in her tone as she bucked into me over and over again. I sucked her clit hard, wanting to squeeze out every last drop of her pleasure. When she lay back, breathless and trembling, I straightened, my hard length still in my hand.

She licked her lips, watching me with hooded eyes as I stroked myself. "Do you want me to—"

"No," I ground out. "Just watch. And make sure I can still see your pretty little pussy."

She spread her legs wider for me and I took in her body, remembering the feel of her as she shook around me. The pace of my strokes increased, my dick so hard it hurt.

When I drew my thumb across her wet clit, she shuddered, sensitive and sated.

And that was it. My balls drew up, and all the tension in my body loosened like a tight cord that had finally frayed and broken apart. My whole body felt like it shattered as hot semen spewed out of me in needy spurts onto the flat of her belly.

I shuddered, loving the rush of release as I looked down at her, my seed on her skin, her hair a wild tangle on the pillow. But when I looked up, she wasn't looking at my cock, wasn't even looking at the mess I'd made on her stomach. She was looking deep into my eyes with complete wonder and adoration.

In that moment, her quiet gaze said more than a mouthful of words ever could. She accepted me just as I was.

God, she's perfect.

When had she become my everything?

Chapter Fourteen

Emma

Placing my hand on the doorknob outside my office, I held my breath, bracing myself for what I knew was waiting for me on the other side. Ignoring the slight ache in my ribs, I pushed the door open and instantly gasped at the sight of my desk.

It was clean—spotless, even. The last time I'd been here, there was a pile of paperwork the size of an algebra textbook in the middle of my desk. I quickly walked behind the desk and started opening drawers, rummaging through each one to see if the cleaning staff had accidentally moved the pile and forgotten to put it back when they were done.

Just as I was starting to get frantic, a soft knock at the door broke me out of my panic. I turned to find Bethany standing there, giving me that mischievous smile I'd come to expect from her.

"Missing something?" she asked, batting her eyelashes.

"Listen, Bethany, if this is some kind of practical

joke, I'm really not in the mood. We're still waiting on a shipment from New York, and if those books don't get here soon, I'll have some *really* angry old ladies to deal with," I said, rubbing the back of my neck in a mix of worry and frustration.

"I took care of it," Bethany chirped, her eyes brightening even more.

I stared at her for a moment and then looked back at my empty desk. "All of it? But that pile was so huge—"

"It's all been handled," she replied, waving her hands in the air as if she were brushing the paperwork away. "Once I knew you'd be okay, I couldn't stand the idea of you defying death by hit-and-run only to drown in a sea of paperwork."

"That was really sweet, but you really didn't have to—"

Bethany cut me off with a hug so tight, I had to keep myself from wincing. "Oh God, your ribs. I'm so sorry!"

She quickly released me and patted my shoulder instead. I smiled and shook my head, taking in a deep breath to ignore the pain in my side.

"I'm just so happy you're back." She smiled at me so big, you'd think I'd just survived a shark attack.

"Me too," I said, looking back at my computer.

"I do have some bad news, though."

A serious look swept over her face. My stomach sank, and I steeled myself for whatever came next.

"Code Brown." She winked. "And it's your turn to handle it."

I sighed and used the rubber band around my wrist to pull my hair back into a ponytail. This wasn't exactly my vision for my triumphant return to work, but hey, at least it was business as usual.

Well, sort of.

Since the death threat and the hit-and-run, Gavin had been more protective than ever. And honestly? It was fucking hot that he'd hired a private investigator to figure out who was behind it all, as well as a driver to take me everywhere I needed to go.

I'd told him that he was overreacting, that I didn't

need so much of his time and energy focused on making sure I was safe. The first part was true. Sure, the death threat and the accident were suspiciously timed, but I hardly thought I was important enough for someone to really be out to kill me. The second part, on the other hand, about not needing so much of his time and energy?

That was a dirty lie.

I loved seeing this new side of him, the one that answered my every beck and call, that made me feel like the most important person on the entire planet. Knowing he had this kind of affectionate side to him made me realize there could be a future for us. A *real* future. If business Gavin wasn't already sexy enough—even despite his need for control—then this new Gavin with a soft side was a freaking fairy tale.

Once I'd finished up the last of my work for the day, I closed up my office and made my way to the parking lot. The private car Gavin arranged for me still felt a little excessive, but it was nice to get home so quickly after a long day at work.

When we arrived at my place, I thanked my driver, nodding as he reminded me that he'd be by in the morning to pick me up. At the door of my beloved brownstone, I reached for the doorknob and was shocked when the door immediately swung open.

Standing inside was a woman about my height, her wavy salt-and-pepper hair just long enough to brush the bottom of her earlobes. She smiled broadly at me, her eyes crinkling softly in the corners, and held her arms out wide to pull me in for a hug.

Oh shit.

"Mom?"

"Hi, sweetie!" My mother squealed, wrapping her arms around me and squeezing so tight, I had to bite my lip to keep from yelping out loud. "I'm so happy to see you."

Gingerly, I hugged her back, patting the space between her shoulders. "Yeah, me too," I said, doing my best to match the enthusiasm in her voice.

After a solid minute, she finally released me, moving her hands to my upper arms and gripping tightly, scanning me like a book she'd just pulled off the shelf. I smiled awkwardly and waited for her to be done searching for any sign of unhappiness or lack of well-being.

"You cut your hair," she said, still giving me that same broad smile.

"I got a trim a few weeks ago, yeah." I nodded, still unsure if she'd ever let me go. "You know, Mom, I always love seeing you. I just wish you would have—" I began, but the crestfallen look on her face cut me off.

"You forgot," she said, dropping her hands to her sides.

Shit, shit, shit.

With all the craziness that had happened in the past few days, I completely forgot that my mom was coming over for dinner tonight. I felt stupid for forgetting, and then frustrated that all that silliness in the hospital had thrown me off so much.

There was no way I could tell her I'd just been in the hospital. If being her only child wasn't bad enough, everything that had happened with Nathan had made her somehow even more protective. My only option was to lie and pretend that things were just crazy at work. Knowing her only daughter had forgotten about their monthly dinner date would hurt my mother, but finding out that someone had hit me with their car? That would just about kill her.

"No, Mom, of course I didn't forget. Things have just been so insane at work, and what with the restorations going on here, I just . . . It slipped my mind, that's all," I said, fumbling my way through the lie.

My mother stared at me for a moment, squinting like she was searching for a diamond earring in a shag carpet. She could tell something was off—I could feel it in her stare—so I smiled and slipped my arm around her waist to lead her to the kitchen.

"Lucky for you," I said, flipping on the light and heading straight for the fridge, "I have all the ingredients for personal pizzas, if you're up for that."

At that, my mother's eyes lit up. Personal pizzas had been a family tradition since I was old enough to sprinkle cheese, and it was the perfect way to smooth things over. *I hope.*

I turned the oven on and pulled out all the

ingredients, smiling as my mom opened a can of black olives, her favorite topping. After popping open the jar of sauce, I sliced up mushrooms, another classic topping on the Bells' famous pizzas. The air between us calmed as my mom and I fell into our familiar routine, and we got right to chatting about everything going on in our lives.

After talking about her new "rosé and romance" book club for a solid ten minutes, my mom turned to give me a quizzical look, raising her eyebrow and suppressing a smile. Before she even said it, I knew what was coming.

"So, sweetie," she said, grating the fresh mozzarella, "what's going on with you? Any new flames I should know about?" Before things had gone south with Nathan, she'd spent months pressing me for grandkids. Apparently, it had been long enough since the end of that relationship for her to start pressing me again.

"Um . . ." I hesitated, unsure how to explain what I had with Gavin—or if I even wanted to.

It was one thing to tell Bethany about every twist and turn in my new roller-coaster relationship. She was worried for me, to be sure, but in the end, she was always supportive of what I wanted. My mom, on the other hand? She had absolutely no qualms about letting me know when she thought I was making a huge mistake.

In that moment, I wished I'd had more time to prepare for this conversation, to practice what I wanted to say. Because, dear God, how did you explain someone like Gavin to your mom?

"Oh, there *is* someone, isn't there? I can see it on your face. Who's the lucky guy, sweetheart? Where did you two meet?" My mom put the mozzarella down at that point, preparing herself for the prospect of grandchildren.

Shit, shit, shit.

"Uh . . . yeah. We, uh, met at a coffee shop," I mumbled, eager to get through this conversation as quickly and painlessly as possible.

"A coffee shop? Wow, how romantic. Did they have some jazz playing on the radio? That stuff always puts me in the mood."

"Oh my God, Mom, ew. Please don't make this about your sex life."

"I'm just saying. And stop changing the subject. Who

is he? What's his name? What does he do for a living?"

My mom's incessant questions and the heat from the oven had started to make me sweat. I fanned myself for a moment before deciding to pull my sweater over my head, grateful for the tank top I had on underneath. As I raised my arms, the hem of my tank top got caught on the fabric of the sweater, exposing my abdomen for a moment before I quickly pulled my tank back down.

I sighed. "His name is Gavin, and before you say anything, I want you to know that I really—"

But before I could finish, my mom was rushing to my side and lifting the hem of my tank top. "What is this?" she whispered, running her fingertips lightly over the bruises on my side.

Shit.

"I'm okay, really," I said, but it was already too late.

With her brows knit closely together, she examined my bruises further, ignoring my efforts to cover them back up with my shirt. She pressed her fingers a little more firmly on one, causing me to step back and wince in pain.

Dirty Little Promise

Mom looked at me, her eyes wide and angry, and shook her head slightly. "Who did this to you?" she murmured, searching my face for answers.

"No one, Mom. I, uh . . . I don't know."

"You don't know? How could you not know?"

"Really, Mom, it's not a big deal."

"Not a big deal? How can you say that to me? After what that monster did to you . . . I thought we were done with this. I thought we'd moved on from men who hit us and hurt us and treat us like nothing." She was pacing now, rubbing her hands over her forearms, her face pinched.

"Mom, what? No, Gavin's not like that."

"Not like that? Sweetheart, look at you. Look at your ribs! I swear, I don't know how you keep finding these men. Your father and I raised you to respect yourself more than this, Emma. We paid for your therapist. I can't believe this is happening again."

"Gavin is *nothing* like Nathan, Mom," I said, raising my voice more than I meant to.

"Really, Emma? Nothing? Then, please, paint me a picture. What does he do? How does he spend his time? Or is that not something he'd want you to tell me?" My mother threw her hands in the air with each question.

"He . . . he runs his own business," I stammered, rubbing my hand over the back of my neck.

"His own business, huh? And what is he selling with this business?"

Damn. How did she always know just the right question to make everything unravel? Maybe it was mother's intuition, but whatever it was, I wasn't comfortable with explaining his company to her.

"He and his brothers . . . they run a, uh, an escort service of sorts," I said, and my mother scoffed and rolled her eyes. "But it's not what you think, Mom, it's not like that. He's not like that."

"Oh, so he's a pimp? What, is he your sugar daddy, or whatever you call it? Is that how you've been able to afford all these renovations?" She gestured around her wildly, pointing at all the work I'd done like I'd sacrificed my soul to do it. "I don't know how you got yourself into

Dirty Little Promise 229

another one of these messes. Your father and I have tried so hard to help you. I don't know if I can handle standing by and watching you get hurt again." She started gathering her things, sliding her arms through the sleeves of her coat and throwing her purse over her shoulder.

"Mom, please, just let me explain," I begged, tears stinging my eyes.

"Maybe another time. This is just . . . too familiar at the moment," she said, pausing at the front door. "I just want you to be safe, Emma." With that, she left, closing the door quietly behind her.

The oven chimed to signal it was adequately preheated, but I wasn't hungry anymore.

I struggled to keep my tears from streaming down my cheeks, and the lump in my throat was getting harder to swallow. I turned the oven off and decided to get some more restoration work done, whether my mom approved of how I got the money for it or not.

Polishing the pewter sconce with an old rag, I pushed a strand of hair out of my face and huffed out a deep breath. I was torn between feeling grateful for the distraction the work provided, and feeling overwhelmed at all the repairs my old brownstone needed. Moving from one stressful issue to the next used to be the kind of thing that centered me, reminded me of how small one problem was in relation to the rest of my life.

But now? Almost everything in my life was stressful, and focusing on a different problem every hour really wasn't helping.

I was already dreading the call I would get from my father the next day, demanding an explanation for my mother's early return home. I had to find a way to calm my parents down so I could explain who Gavin was and how important he was quickly becoming to me. It would be a tricky conversation, made even harder by the unanswered questions even I still had. Maybe if my parents could just meet him, they would see how wrong my mother's assumptions about him were. I knew it. I felt it.

On the surface, sure, the two men seemed to share some alpha-male tendencies. But if you dug a little deeper?

Gavin and Nathan couldn't be more different.

Chapter Fifteen

Gavin

The minute Emma was granted a clean bill of health, Cooper packed up his things and left. It was an unceremonious departure—he didn't even bother to stop by my door before he'd gone. But when the door shut behind him, there was no doubting things were different around the office.

Quinn never said a word about the change, never chastised me for my actions or accused me of pushing Cooper out, but I still felt a twinge of guilt every time I thought of my younger brother. For Emma, sacrifices had had to be made. It was just unfortunate that Cooper was one of them.

Now, though, I couldn't help but wonder if it was for the best. There was a new weight on my shoulders, one I had no idea how to lift. It made me wonder if it might be beneficial for everyone I loved to stay as far away from them as possible. But he wasn't gone for good, he'd made that clear—he was just scouting out some possible locations. A decision on where he'd end up would come later.

I pushed the thought away, determined to deal with that another day. Tonight wasn't about Cooper or my problems. Now that Emma was well again, I wanted to take her out to celebrate.

I'd already pulled out all my favorite stops with her before. The vineyard, the helicopter, whisking her away to a beach getaway—well, sort of. That trip was actually for work. Everything I'd planned for her so far had been an invitation into my world, so this date had to be about hers.

What the fuck do bookworms like to do besides read? I racked my brain for options.

Take her to a nice bookstore? *She works in a damn library.*

Track down her favorite author and arrange a meeting? *No, I want this to be about her and me, not some third wheel.*

Fly her to the museum of typewriters? *Right, because nothing says "let's fuck" like a bunch of dusty, outdated writing machines.*

Jesus, Gavin, use your fucking head.

For a second, I considered calling Emma. I could ask about her wildest dream, then make it come true in a heartbeat. She would love it, would practically turn to putty in my hands.

And she would see it coming from a mile away.

No, this had to be special, completely from me.

In the past, I would have asked Sonja what I should do, but since that option was now gone, I buzzed Alyssa and waited until she opened my office door.

"You rang?" she asked, her eyebrows raised in annoyance.

"I did. Come in."

She stepped inside and clicked the door shut behind her. Taking a seat opposite me, she crossed her legs and tilted her head to the side. "What is it?"

"I need your help."

"I gathered as much," she said, and if I didn't know her better, I'd think her tone was almost testy.

"I wanted to take Emma on a nice date, but I can't

figure out where."

"Your name can get you into any restaurant in the city. Are you seriously interrupting my workday for this?"

I gave her a warning glare. "It needs to be more special than that."

"Why? Going to propose?"

I paused, my heart skipping at the idea. "No. It just needs to be a special night. Something that only Emma would appreciate."

"So, something that showcases your sense of humor?" Alyssa asked.

"Why do I ask you anything?" I shot back with an eye roll.

"Because without me, your life would fall apart. Look, I don't know. She's a bookworm, right? Can't you take her to see the old Shakespeare manuscripts in the library? Or isn't there some really pretentious bookstore you could go to?"

I sat up straighter in my chair. "Alyssa, you're a genius."

"This is why you pay me a very handsome salary," she said. "Now, what else do you need?"

"That's all."

Rolling her eyes, she got up from the chair and left my office, but I barely paid any attention to her. I had an idea, and that was all I needed.

Grateful for her help, I made a mental note to buy Alyssa a box of excellent chocolates. But before I could dig into some research for tonight, she peeked back inside my office.

"Sorry to interrupt, but I have a Mr. Huntington waiting to speak to you on line two."

Fuck.

Squeezing my hand into a fist, I took a slow, deep breath before relaxing again. I picked up the phone, wedging it between my ear and shoulder so I could quickly jot down as much as I could remember.

"Fine, put him on," I growled.

I had little patience for whatever idiotic complaint

this client had to offer, but with Cooper gone, I didn't have much of a choice. He had always been the schmoozer, quick to agree with clients and find an immediate solution. He liked people and understood how important it was to keep them happy.

Me, on the other hand? It took every ounce of my self-control to keep from telling half these whiny morons to shove it and be grateful for the quality of arm candy our company was able to provide.

Yeah, we really needed to find someone else to handle customer relations.

"Gavin, I'm not transferring the call until you promise not to offend him," Alyssa said, her tone sharp and resolute.

"I will be the epitome of an ass-kisser," I said in the flattest tone possible.

I could practically hear Alyssa rolling her eyes through the phone. "Gavin."

"Yes, fine. I'll play nice."

Alyssa didn't respond, just silently transferred the

call. I shifted in my seat, leaning back in my chair to get more comfortable.

"This is Gavin Kingsley. How can I help you today, Mr. Huntington?"

"Gavin? I need to speak with your brother. He promised to make special accommodations for me before my next event, and I have yet to receive confirmation that they will indeed be fulfilled."

I rolled my eyes. "If you need to speak with Quinn, I can have my assistant transfer you momentarily."

"No, no, your other brother. Cooper. I was promised a platinum blonde in a holographic dress, and I'll be damned if you send me a brunette."

Pinching the bridge of my nose with my free hand, I clenched my jaw to keep from sighing loudly. *Cooper, what the fuck?*

"Absolutely, Mr. Huntington. I'll be sure all your needs are met." After a few more moments of playing along, I transferred the call back to Alyssa, explaining what needed to be done.

I slammed down the phone, then leaned back in my chair and ran my hands over my face. Fucking Cooper. Always willing to go the extra mile.

I needed a break. Better yet, I needed to get laid. And since Emma had been practically begging for it when I last saw her, I was willing to bet that she did too.

My cock twitched at the thought, all the more reason to make tonight special.

• • •

When the workday was over, I headed to the library to pick up Emma. When I arrived, she was already trudging from the building, looking tired and weary after her second day back at work.

I crossed the street toward her and swept her into my arms, kissing her neck and making her laugh.

"What are you doing here?" she asked.

"I missed you. Did you have a rough day?"

She sighed. "That would be an understatement. I love Bethany for trying, but the library I came back to wasn't the same one I left a week ago. Anyway, I've sorted out the chaos. What are you doing here? Still trying to make sure nobody hits me with their car?"

"No." I shook my head. "Well, yes, but that's not my primary concern. I came to surprise you. Come on."

I slipped my hand in hers and led her to my car. Today, I'd opted not to have Ben with us. I wanted it to be a private night. Intimate. Just her and me.

When I opened the passenger side door, she glanced down and furrowed her brow at the large white dress box in her seat.

"What's this?" she asked.

"A present. Open it."

She did as I asked and offered me a weak smile as her fingers trailed the blue chiffon cocktail dress.

"What's the matter?" I asked.

"I love it. It's perfect and beautiful."

"But?"

She pursed her lips. "It's nothing. Thank you."

I fell silent for a moment, wondering if she was thinking about how Cooper used to send her gowns to wear before their dates, like I suddenly was. Even in another state, he cast a shadow over our relationship.

"I'll go back in and change. I'll be right back out."

She took the dress in hand and I trailed her across the street, waiting on the library steps as she went back inside.

When Emma reappeared, every thought of Cooper was swept away. She was too gorgeous to focus on anything other than the way the cocktail dress hugged her perfect curves and brought out the color of her eyes.

"You look stunning," I said.

"This is a great surprise." She grinned. "Thank you."

Together, we made our way back to the car, and I revved the Mercedes' engine before turning onto the street back into the city.

As I drove, she smiled, studying me. "You know, this whole time I thought you couldn't drive."

"What?" I laughed.

"You always have Ben drive us. I thought you didn't know how."

I shook my head. "I like to keep Ben on the payroll, that's all. I'm in a position to put people in jobs, so that's what I want to do."

Her smile softened. "That's sweet. Now tell me, where are we going?"

"It's a surprise."

Emma badgered me with questions about our surprise date the whole ride over, her constant pleading and arm waving making her breasts sway in a way I couldn't argue with. She looked gorgeous, as always, but something about how the low-cut scoop neck-dress she had on hugged her curves in all the right places had my mind spinning with thoughts of what I would do to her later.

When we arrived at the venue, Emma's eyes grew large.

"The Italics Lounge," she murmured, arching one of her eyebrows at me. "Aren't they hosting an erotic poetry reading tonight?" She blushed at the word *erotic*, dipping her chin so her long, dark hair fell across half of her face.

I reached out to brush her hair out of her eyes before lifting her chin with two fingers. "I wanted to please you tonight," I murmured.

She smiled demurely, softly licking her supple lower lip. "You have."

I ushered Emma out of the car, giving her perfect ass a swift pat as she climbed out. She turned and shot me a look so sexy, I had to pause for a moment to calm down before exiting the vehicle.

We walked into the lounge just minutes before the start of the reading. I grabbed us each a glass of bubbly from the bar before joining Emma at our reserved table near the front.

A tall, redheaded woman with long, skinny arms and an impressive rack sat under a single spotlight in the middle of the stage. Her stool was just high enough for one foot to dangle in the air while the other steadied her on the floor. She wore a tight red dress with a plunging neckline that barely held in her cleavage. She was beautiful, for sure, but even in the spotlight, she paled in comparison to Emma.

"My name is Heather, and I'll be reading from my new collection," the redheaded woman purred, her voice breathy and rhythmic. "If you're interested, I'll be selling books in the back after my set."

Emma turned to raise her eyebrows at me, and I slipped my hand onto her knee in response. I rubbed my thumb over the hem of her dress, lightly brushing the skin underneath. She smiled coyly at me before crossing her legs, pulling her knee out of my reach.

"You'll pay for that later," I growled, my cock twitching at the thought.

Emma didn't respond, simply tossed her hair over her shoulder and placed her finger over her mouth to shush me. Heather Ruble was beginning.

"If I could live with you inside me forever," Heather said, her voice breathy, "we would move through the world in perfect pleasure, swimming in wave after wave of ecstasy . . . ohhh," she said, punctuating the line with a moan.

The woman continued reciting her poem from memory, moving her hands gracefully through the air. Her voice was enticing, low and velvety smooth. But from the corner of my eye, I could see Emma's chest heaving with arousal at each line of poetry. Suddenly, all I could think about was how wet she would be by the end of this night.

Heather's reading ended, and she was followed by two more poets whose work was equally stimulating. One was a woman who included subtle moans and "ohs" in her poetry, mimicking the sound of an orgasm. The other was a man who described the shape of his lover so vividly, it made my own heart pound—and I didn't think I was into this kind of thing. But there was no denying it was enticing.

By the end of the readings, I wanted nothing more than to find a decent alleyway nearby and ravage Emma then and there. With the erotic poems swimming through my mind, it was nearly impossible to think about anything else.

But there was no way in hell I'd let my hours of planning go to waste.

After leaving the Italics Lounge, I took Emma to a

coffee shop similar to the one we used to frequent. Books and tea, two of her favorite things in one night.

The night scene at this place was exactly what I'd hoped for—low lighting, hushed tones, and soft jazz playing in the background. I bought a slice of chocolate cake for us to share. We were silent as we began to eat, the air between us practically crackling with sexual tension. She moaned softly after her first bite, making my cock twitch in response.

"Which was your favorite reading?" I asked, finally breaking the silence.

"Mmm . . . the second one, I think," Emma replied, her eyes so dark with lust, I could hardly take it any longer.

I nodded, taking another bite of the cake in an effort to calm the pulsing in my pants.

"It was so erotic, I was starting to get a little turned on," she purred, and I nearly dropped my fork.

"Come with me," I ordered, grabbing her hand.

I didn't care anymore about finishing the date, the

cake, any of it. It was time to be alone.

Once in the car, I crushed my mouth against hers, running my hands over her thighs. My dick was getting harder by the minute. I swept my fingers over her panties, groaning at how wet I could feel they'd become. I needed to be inside her, needed to feel her warmth pulsing around my cock.

But first I had to drive us home.

I barely kept the car between the lines with the scent of Emma drowning out all my senses. She was so beautiful, so stunning, and I'd waited long enough to have her.

Back at my place, I decided to take things up a notch. Or ten.

The moment we stepped inside the front door, I removed Emma's dress and swept her legs up and around my waist. She gasped and clung to me tightly, which only made me want her more. Landing a series of hungry kisses all over her neck and chest, I walked us to my bedroom, each step pressing my cock closer to her needy pussy.

After throwing her onto her back on the bed, I began

to slowly remove my shirt, reveling in the sight of her slender body moving with desire. Emma propped herself up on her elbows, her supple breasts swaying with the motion. Her eyes locked on the massive bulge in my pants, and she began inching her way to the edge of the bed. Tossing my shirt to the floor, I grabbed her ankles and pulled her toward me, nodding toward my erection.

"Take out my cock," I growled.

She greedily unbuckled my belt, her swift fingers unfastening and opening my pants. Within moments, she pulled out all nine inches, her eyes still as wide and appreciative as the first time she saw me. Emma leaned forward to take me in her mouth but I stepped back, causing her to look up at me with questioning eyes.

"No. I have something else in mind," I said, kicking my pants off.

I pushed her onto her back, running my tongue over the length of her abdomen, pausing just short of her rosy nipple. She moaned softly and shifted her hips under me, her pretty pink pussy glistening in the dim light of the moon.

I descended on her breast, taking her nipple in my mouth with a gentle, teasing bite. Emma gasped and wrapped her fingers around the back of my neck, grabbing a fistful of my hair.

As I swirled my tongue around her breast, I reached between her legs and began stroking her wet, swollen lips. Alternating between pumping two fingers and massaging her clit, I watched in wonder as she cried out, her hips rocking with my motions.

She was radiant and wild, and I knew she was ready for what I'd planned for us next.

I flipped her over onto her stomach and continued fingering her from behind, enjoying the view of her perfect ass. I took a handful of one cheek in my hand, massaging it roughly, and let out a growl.

"So fucking sexy."

She responded by lifting it higher in the air. I reached over to my bedside table, rummaging through the drawer for a bottle of special oil I kept there.

I drew her up on her knees, her face still buried in a pillow. With her round ass lifted high in the air like that, all ready and expectant to take everything I had to give? I couldn't help it. My palm landed with a thwack right in the center of one of her cheeks, causing Emma to whimper in a way that made my entire body throb.

I lubricated my fingertips with a small amount of the oil. When I closed the lid with a soft click, Emma turned her head onto the other cheek and said, "I'm already so wet," wiggling her hips in the air.

"Yes, you are," I murmured, thrusting two fingers inside her.

She moaned and pressed her hips back against my hand, urging me to go deeper. I pumped my fingers in and out, running my thumb over the rosebud between her cheeks.

"But this isn't for your pussy."

Emma paused, her hips now motionless as she processed my proposition. I waited for her reply, my needy cock growing more impatient by the second.

She slid her hips forward and flipped herself over, propping up on her elbows as she looked at me with worried eyes. "I . . . I don't think I'm ready for that," she said, dropping her gaze and turning her face to the side.

I nodded and lifted her chin, needing to look in her eyes. "Tell me why."

"I—I'm afraid it will hurt," she admitted softly.

"Have you done it before?"

She nodded. "Sort of. I mean, I tried to. Nathan made me . . ."

If I thought I hated her ex before, this new level of hatred and disgust was magnified tenfold. I wanted to rip out his throat with my bare hands for making this beautiful girl feel unsure and afraid.

She looked away again, refusing to meet my gaze. I knew that feeling—of not wanting to show any weakness, not wanting to admit your fears but needing desperately to be stronger. It was a push and pull I'd felt often as I worked through my own inner battles over the years.

Leaning down over her, bringing my face close to hers, I whispered, "I would never, ever do anything to hurt you. You know that, right?"

She nodded slowly, her eyes falling closed.

"Only want to bring you pleasure," I murmured, pressing my lips against her throat, loving the soft, feminine scent of her skin, the way her pulse jumped in response to my touch.

Emma sighed, bringing her arms around me. "I know that. In my head. I do, I swear. But I'm just . . ."

"In time," I said, encouraging her.

She nodded, smiling softly, her pert breasts nodding with her. "Is it a control thing for you? Wanting to take me *there*, I mean?"

I weighed her question, letting out a slow exhale. "Partly." Then I smirked at her, a wicked smile, and her own mouth twitched. "Plus, it'll feel really fucking good." My teeth grazed the side of her neck. "For both of us."

Emma shivered in my arms, and I knew the time for talking was done. I needed to erase the painful memory of what her cruel ex-boyfriend had done to her, and I would, but that would be another time. Right now, I just wanted to push into her and hear her cry out my name in that soft, breathy whimper that I found so utterly sexy.

Drawing her body close, I aligned my cock between her legs, and ever so slowly buried myself in her tight heat, causing her to gasp and tremble. She felt so good, so right, so perfect, and I'd missed this—so fucking much. Despite my desire to go slow, I started fucking her with rough, quick thrusts, grasping her hips for support as I tugged her body down onto mine. Again. And again.

Her breathing quickened, her moans more frequent, and just as I brought her to the brink of climax, I stopped. I pulled out and began entering her very slowly, one tantalizing inch at a time.

As Emma squirmed beneath me, trying to pull me fully inside her, I dipped my head close to hers to whisper all the dirty things she would give me—and soon.

Chapter Sixteen

Emma

This was heaven.

Gavin's firm body on mine, the weight of him balanced precariously over me.

His hips thrusting powerfully as he rocked into me.

Pleasure skyrocketing through my veins.

He'd surprised me tonight by asking about taking me *there*. Of course, I wanted to please him, wanted to show him that I was stronger than my past. I wasn't going to let a few bad experiences tarnish the fun I knew we could have.

But he'd respected my decision and didn't push it any further. His understanding and quiet acceptance made me feel all soft and squishy inside.

As Gavin continued thrusting into me, driving us both deeper into pleasure, I was struck with an idea. Just because I wasn't willing to try *that* didn't mean I wasn't game for something else. If he wanted something different tonight, that was something I could give him. If only he'd ease back on his strict control and let me.

"Gavin?" I groaned.

Rather than respond, he reached out and pinched my nipple, sending a wave of pleasure and pain so sharp through me that I nearly came right then and there.

"I want to be on top," I whispered, trying a more direct approach.

Without another word, he pulled back and sat in the center of the bed. He looked so sexy with his muscled chest and abs, and his legs spread apart so I could see every inch of his powerful muscled thighs.

"You want to ride this cock? Show me," he demanded.

I didn't need to be told twice.

Hardly breathing, I climbed into his lap, straddled him, and gripped him with one hand as I led him to the space between my thighs. Slowly, I rolled his throbbing head over my tight bundle of nerves, groaning at the insistent push and pull of pleasure and tension his heat created. But still, it wasn't enough.

Wanting to make this good for him, I swirled him around the outside of my opening, watching his eyes as I moved slowly, slowly.

"Jesus," he grunted.

And then I lowered myself, inch by glorious inch, as deep as I could take him.

Bracing my hands on his shoulders, I anchored myself against him as I tested moving up then down, first teasing his head and then dropping lower until he was finally buried to the hilt.

A deep groan of satisfaction rumbled in his chest. "You're so tight against me," he ground out.

"Too tight?" I asked, suddenly unsure if he was experiencing pleasure or actual pain.

"Never. You're utterly fucking perfect."

It was slow and torturous for both of us, the rising need and then the instant of relief before it was torn away again, but it was driving me to the edge.

I threw my head back as I arched again, pushing my

breasts toward his waiting mouth, and he licked each swell before finding my nipple and sucking hard and deep.

Finally, I couldn't hold back any longer. I rocked harder, faster, needing to feel him deep and thick inside me. Needing to feel the way his cock twitched as he spiraled closer and closer to the brink with me.

This was everything, and when he finally groaned my name, I knew I had his permission.

With a low cry, I broke apart as the tightly coiled tension inside me spread into ecstasy. He gripped my hips and plunged deeper into me as my body clenched and shuddered around him.

He was coming with me , I knew it, but I was so wrapped up in my own waves of pleasure that I could hardly think. Distantly, I heard him cry my name. And when I finally managed to meet his gaze again, I saw what I was feeling reflected back at me.

He might not know it yet, might not be ready to admit it, but he loved me. Gavin Kingsley loved me, and nothing could stop us now.

After we made love, Gavin held me quietly in his

strong arms until I drifted off to that space that was one stop short of sleep. Being here with him in his bed, our naked limbs intertwined beneath the sheets, I couldn't help but think about how far he'd come since the beginning—when he practically kicked me out immediately after sex.

I was so thankful for all the changes in him, so thankful that he was mine and I was his.

It gave me comfort to provide what he needed. Did it mean I was merely a vessel for his pleasure, that I lost my spirit and sense of self? No, quite the opposite. Being his was a powerful thing—and it wasn't for the faint of heart.

He stroked my hair, gazing down at me. "Good girl. You made me very happy tonight."

His praise was everything. It was hard earned, and I couldn't help but take a second and enjoy this tender moment.

He was changing. We were changing. I should have felt tentative and slightly fearful. Change was often scary. Instead, this was exhilarating. This growth in him was everything I'd ever dreamed about.

Gathering my courage, I opened my mouth to speak the words to him I'd held in for the last several weeks.

"What is it?" Gavin asked, smirking at me. It must have been obvious I had something on my mind.

"I know we haven't fully defined this," I said, starting slowly.

"Yes, we have. You're my person, remember?"

I nodded. "That's true." Nerves rolled through my belly, but I pressed on. "But for me, it's more. I have these big, mushy feelings for you. I'm crazy about you."

"I feel the same way, pet. You're everything to me."

"I love you, Gavin," I blurted. "And I just wanted to tell you. You don't have to say it back just because I said it, but I wanted you to know how I felt. I couldn't hold it in any longer."

His lips parted, and for a moment, he didn't say anything. "Oh, pet. My brave girl." He stroked my hair, then patted my cheek. "Thank you for telling me."

But he didn't return the sentiment. In fact, he didn't say anything else for several long moments while the deafening silence in the room settled around us until my skin felt itchy and tight.

"Come here. Let me hold you," he breathed against my hair, and I took a deep breath and let him fold me into his arms.

I hated his stony silence, hated the question mark lingering between us, but I couldn't bring myself to regret telling him. I did love him. So much it hurt.

A short time later, I woke alone in bed. Gavin's side of the bed was cool, and missing his body heat, the need to go hunt for him was a necessity. I knew I wouldn't be able to fall back asleep without his firm, muscled body next to mine.

Dressed in Gavin's discarded button-down shirt, I made my way from the bedroom in search of him. The soft glow of lamplight drew me to his office. I leaned against the doorway, my shirt unbuttoned, hoping I could tempt him back to bed.

"Everything okay?" I asked.

When his weary eyes lifted to meet mine, I didn't like the stress I saw there, the worry. Unsure what was on his mind, I crossed the room and knelt at his feet. My king.

He reached for my cheek and offered me a sad smile. "Everything's fine," he assured me.

I didn't believe him. "Tell me, Gavin. Please. You can trust me." I leaned into his touch as my stomach tensed, hoping that my declaration earlier hadn't freaked him out. *Please, God, don't let it be that.*

He petted my hair. "I know I can. But honestly, it's nothing I want you to worry over. We're just under a bit of pressure to hire a replacement for Sonja."

While that was probably true, I doubted that was what had pushed him out of bed in the middle of the night.

"Can I help? Get your mind off things, I mean?"

He didn't respond, just tilted his head as he watched me. I placed my hand over the bulge in his black boxer briefs, stroking him softly until I coaxed his manhood awake.

Gavin turned his chair from the desk to face me, tugging his boxers down just enough to free himself, but didn't say a word.

I soothed him the only way I knew he'd allow. Afterward, he laced our fingers together and led me back to bed.

Chapter Seventeen

Gavin

I pulled the copy of the subpoena from my briefcase and slid it across the desk to my stern-faced lawyer. So far, he was the only person I'd managed to bring myself to tell. Not my brothers.

Not even Emma.

He perched a pair of thick-framed glasses on the edge of his nose and his eyes zoomed back and forth, reading the words I now knew by heart.

"I don't understand. It's been two years," I muttered under my breath.

He held up a finger as he finished reading the last page, and sat the papers down before folding his hands on his desk. "Mr. Kingsley, I'm going to be blunt. This is a cash grab, and frankly, I'm not surprised. Your company has been in the papers for a couple of weeks now, and the value of it has been printed in every newspaper in North America."

"So? Anyone with a *Forbes* magazine or an Internet browser could've learned that."

His salt-and-pepper mustache twitched, and he let out a long, slow sigh. "Yes, and once they did, they decided to come after you."

I glanced at the document between us. "Their daughter died years ago."

He shook his head. "Exactly. It's likely they had no idea how much you were worth back then. And you and I both know that number has increased tenfold in the interim."

"But the statute of limitations—"

"Is six years in civil cases like this. If Ashley's family can prove, as they assert, that you were the cause of leading their daughter down a path to drugs and debauchery, they can still find you liable."

"That's so wrong." I'd spent every day since her death blaming myself. And now, just when I was finally ready to move on with my life, to let love in and forgive myself? This happened.

"It is, and they'll never win." He spread his hands wide. "But they don't need to. All they have to do is sit down with the press and add to your troubles. This story getting out, with the finger pointed at you as the cause, would be the death blow for your business. They expect you to settle. Pay to make the problem go away."

"Those bastards."

I'd only met her parents once—her mom was a gold-digging drunk, and her father was a heartless businessman. That had been my impression at the time, and now it seemed I was correct. They'd fostered her as a teen, adopting her officially right before her eighteenth birthday. I knew Ashley didn't love them. And somehow, I knew they didn't love her. They saw her as some project, a charity case they could flaunt to their socialite inner circle and then pat themselves on the back.

With every word, my temper was rising. I could hardly believe it when I'd first gotten the documents with the news that Ashley's family was suing me for her wrongful death. It made no sense.

I wasn't her drug dealer. I wasn't her doctor.

I was her boyfriend.

And as far as I could tell, I'd been the only person

she'd had in the world.

No one but me had cared that Ashley was suffering, that she needed help. I was the one who stood by her, who paid for her treatment. And in the end, I was the one who paid for her funeral.

Even then, on that rainy, terrible day, they did what they'd always done when she was alive—nothing. They simply stood by her graveside, watching as she was lowered into the plot they hadn't paid for, both of them dry-eyed.

"You have a choice to make, Mr. Kingsley. You can try to fight this, or you can settle and get it over with. But I would advise you to consider how it will affect your business and your livelihood if you go to court. The bad press would almost certainly be the final nail in your coffin."

I swallowed the rage threatening to choke me. He wasn't saying anything I hadn't already considered in the days since this letter had come. Still, to hear it out loud . . .

"So, you think I should settle?" I asked.

He shrugged. "I think you should do what's best for you and your company. If I were you, I would settle. But again, I'm not you."

"Thank you. I'll think it over and will give you a call."

The lawyer nodded, and I shook his hand before heading back onto the city streets and gulping down a deep breath of air.

Slowly, I reached for my cell phone and turned it to silent, needing a break from the world around me, a chance to clear my head. Because, truth be told, I knew he was right. If I let this case go to trial, it could ruin me. Could ruin everyone and everything.

Quinn. Cooper. Our employees. And the fragile new start I'd forged with Emma.

God, she'd said she loved me. Her words spoken with such conviction had gutted me, had sliced right through my heart. And while I hadn't returned her words, the possibility of it had been weighing on my mind.

I headed back to my apartment, changed clothes, and went to the nearest park. With the wind on my face and the sun in my eyes, it was easier to breathe, to think. To ignore the steady heartbeat of fury at the people who had denied Ashley and now were trying to ruin me, all for trying my damnedest to save a girl who hadn't wanted to be saved.

Closing my eyes for a second, I relished the cool wind on my skin as I reached the cobblestone path and broke into an easy run.

What kind of man would I be to settle, though? What would it say to the world if I gave Ashley's parents all that money, effectively admitting that I was in the wrong? I would look like a murderer, at worst, and an abuser at best.

I couldn't allow it. My lawyer wanted me to focus on not ruining the company, but having someone at the helm who'd practically admitted to murder would surely ruin the company if the press got wind of it.

Which meant I was going to fight.

And at the end of it all?

I was going to win.

I had to, or it might cost me everything. Including

my sweet, precious Emma, and there was no way I was giving up the best thing in my life without a fight. Somehow, I knew—she'd never hurt me, never cheat, never disappoint. Never let me go. I just knew. Or, at least, I prayed it to be true. I wasn't a religious man, but in that moment, I wanted to be.

I was in love with my sexy little librarian, and though it scared the ever-loving fuck out of me, I was determined to find a way to make this all work.

Ever since the words had left her lips, I could see it whenever she looked at me, whenever she touched me. At first, I'd wanted to pull back, but then I realized that what I felt for her was more than just lust too. The more time I spent with her, the more I felt like she was becoming a part of me. Like she was half of something inside me that was only complete when she was near.

I'd never felt that way, not even with Ashley. But even as good as it felt on the one hand, on the other it was like a looming darkness, hovering over me as I waited for it to come to a tragic end.

Just like everything in my life always seemed to.

Chapter Eighteen

Emma

I was having the sexiest dream about Gavin. One that was just getting to the good part when my phone chirped and I reached for the bedside table, not bothering to open my eyes as I fumbled for the phone.

It was daylight, but only just barely. Either way, it was too early for this, especially on the weekend. Gavin turned beside me and mumbled something I couldn't understand as I thumbed the glass screen and glanced at my messages.

"Crap," I muttered, flopping back onto the bed with a groan as the last of my sexy dream evaporated in the harsh light of day.

"What? What's wrong?" Gavin sat up in bed and eyed me, his brows pinched with concern. He'd had so much on his plate lately, and the last few days it had really seem to hit him. He looked exhausted. And it hardly seemed like the right time to dump this on him, but damn it, it wasn't going to go away, either.

"Nothing, nothing. Go back to sleep," I said, but my

stomach clenched as I tried to think of how to broach the subject.

"Talk to me. Is it work stuff?"

I sighed, tucking the sheets around me as I sat up alongside him, fluffing my pillow behind me. "You remember how I told you my mom came into the city for a day trip after the . . . after the accident?"

Gavin nodded.

"Well, now she's claiming that she had such a good time on her visit that she already wants to see me again. And this time, she's bringing my dad." I rolled my eyes.

"So?" He shrugged. "That's not so bad, right? You told me you get along well with your parents."

"I do, it's just . . ." I blew out another long sigh and squeezed my eyes closed.

"There's something else," Gavin said.

I nodded, forcing myself to meet his gaze. "They want to meet you."

He raised his eyebrows. "Oh."

I studied his face, and while he seemed slightly taken aback, he hadn't gotten up to run in the other direction. Yet.

I'd talked to my mother only once since she'd visited my place and had flipped out over my bruised ribs. I had to set her straight so she knew Gavin wasn't responsible for the marks on my body. I told her everything—that we'd called the police, that Gavin had hired a private investigator and insisted on hiring me a driver so I wouldn't take the bus anymore. When I was done, she'd softened, saying she was happy about that. But we hadn't really talked more about my relationship with him, or about the man himself. And I had a feeling today she was going to grill us both.

"I can make up an excuse if you don't want to go. Really, it's not a big deal," I rushed to assure him. "They sprang this on me and—"

"When do they want to meet me?" he asked, tucking his arm behind his head in a motion that made his biceps bulge in the most delicious way.

"Uh . . . today," I said, forcing that stubborn dream

out of my mind again and focusing back on his face. "For lunch, actually."

"Shit. What time is it?"

"Ten." I groaned. "So, we'd have to start getting ready, like, now."

He reached for his phone on the other bedside table as he morphed into all-business, take-control Gavin. "That's okay. I'll call the Plaza and see if we can get a table—"

"No, no, no." I waved my hands frantically. "Nothing fancy. My parents aren't fancy people, and they're going to want to pay."

Gavin frowned. "But that's ridiculous. I can cover it."

"I know you can cover it, and they probably do too. That's not the point. Look, it'll hurt my dad's pride if you pay. Let's just go to some touristy chain restaurant. That should be fine."

As if any of it would be fine. My mother had made her feelings perfectly clear. I could only hope this invite was exactly what it seemed to be. An olive branch, her way of telling me she was willing to get to know Gavin before she passed judgment. God, I hoped so.

I gnawed at my thumbnail as I wondered if she'd told my dad what Gavin did for a living. He studied me for a long moment before a slow smile spread over his face.

"What?" I demanded.

"You're cute when you're nervous."

"I'm not nervous. I'm just . . ." I couldn't find the words. "I just want this to go well. You're, you know, important to me. I want my parents to see that."

"You're important to me too, Emma."

I sensed there was more he wanted to say, holding my gaze with his and smiling down at me. But then the moment passed.

"So, is there anything I should know then, to make this easier for you?" Gavin asked.

I thought hard. "My dad likes the Steelers, but he's never been to Pittsburgh or any part of Pennsylvania."

Gavin laughed.

"And whatever you do, don't encourage my mother to tell stories about me as a kid. She loves to embarrass me, and she has no qualms about telling you anything."

"Noted." He nodded. "But that only serves as an enticement, to be honest."

I yanked the pillow from behind my head and covered my face with it. "I thought you wanted to make this easy on me."

"Easy, but not a breeze." He chuckled, tugging the pillow away and pressing a kiss to my forehead. "Besides, I want to hear stories about you when you were little. You were probably adorable."

"Trust me, you don't," I warned. "And I wasn't. I was a pain in the ass. Sort of like how you're being right now."

Gavin held up his hands in mock surrender. "Fine, no prying questions. Got it. What else?"

He was grinning now, and I kept going because this was the first time in days that the worry line between his eyes had smoothed. If my misery was what it took to make him this carefree, I was willing to take the bullet.

"What else? Oh!" I snapped my fingers. "Don't order a bottle of wine for the table. My mother will drink the entire thing by herself, regardless of the time of day or type of wine."

"Don't worry so much, baby." He got up from the bed, letting the sheets fall away from him to reveal his naked form.

Even after so long, I couldn't help that my breath caught at the sight at him. I found myself staring at his stiff morning wood, wondering exactly how much time we had to kill before meeting my parents.

"Want to continue this conversation in the shower?" He raised his eyebrows, then crossed the bed toward me and pulled away the covers. Gently, he tweaked one of my nipples and bent to nip at my bottom lip. "I get awful lonely in there by myself."

In the space of an instant, I found myself completely at his mercy. Worries forgotten, I took his hand and allowed him to lead me into the next room and then into the spray of the warm water.

The euphoria of our time together was short-lived, though. By the time we got out of the shower, I found another text blinking on my phone—instructions to meet my parents at a family-style Italian chain they frequented at home that served unlimited salad and breadsticks.

I typed a quick reply and spun around to face Gavin. "What do I do? I wore the last of the clothes I had here last night. Do we stop at my place? We have to be at the restaurant in—"

"Breathe, baby. Calm down." He laid a steadying hand on my shoulder. "I'll steam your dress and get the wrinkles out. You didn't wear it for very long." He winked.

"I can't do that."

"Why not?"

"Because . . ." I dropped my voice to a whisper. "What if they can tell we had sex when I was wearing it?"

"You forgot to mention they were superheroes." Gavin raised an eyebrow. "Impressive."

"Don't get cute."

"Can't help it. But, seriously, the only people who will know are you and me. Promise."

Still unsure, I remembered my work clothes that I still had in my overnight bag. I gave those to Gavin to steam instead, while I applied what little makeup I had rolling around in the bottom of my purse.

• • •

Somehow, we managed to get ready and to the restaurant on time. When we walked through the wide glass doors, I found my parents waiting at the first table inside, a bottle of white wine already on the table directly in front of my mother.

"Oh crap," I grumbled, but Gavin ignored me. Instead, he offered my parents his widest, warmest smile and extended his hand to each of them.

"It's so good to meet you. Thank you for the invitation," he said, and though my parents both smiled back, they looked strained, and I could see the determination in their eyes.

That's when it hit me like a ton of bricks.

This wasn't lunch, it was an inquisition. And poor Gavin was the target.

"It's such a pleasure to meet you too, Mr. Kingsley," my father said coolly.

"Gavin, please." He pulled out my chair and helped me into it before taking his own seat. At this, my mother raised her eyebrows and shot me a skeptical glance over the rim of her wineglass, as if to say, *Aren't we trying too hard?*

My cheeks heated, but I took Gavin's hand and gave it a squeeze.

"I was telling your father about how well the renovations are going on Nana's house, dear," my mom said with a smile.

"Thanks." I grinned, relieved at the neutral topic. "I'm proud of it."

"She's done such a great job putting the place together," Gavin added. "It must mean a lot to both of you to have the house preserved that way."

My father nodded, his expression guarded. "My mother was meticulous about that house. I'm sure she'd be happy to have it in the family still."

My mother smiled her agreement. "What about you, Gavin? Are you close to your grandparents?"

I frowned, glancing at Gavin. I should have prepared him for this. They'd want to know about his family, his background.

To my surprise, he seemed completely unfazed by the question. He squeezed my hand and said, "No, I never met them. It's just me and my brothers."

"I'm sorry to hear that," my mother offered stiffly as she glanced at her menu.

"Don't be. I'm very lucky to have my siblings. But I don't want to monopolize the conversation. As I understand it, you have some amazing stories about Emma growing up that I have to hear."

I pinched him under the table, but his poker face never slipped. Here I was, worried about him, and he was throwing me under the bus. My cheeks heated as I silently plotted my revenge.

Regardless of my feelings on the topic, though, it was the perfect play. My mother's face lit up and she leaned forward in her chair.

"Well, since you asked . . ."

She launched into a story she'd told roughly a million times before, one where I lifted my dress at kindergarten graduation and showed the entire school my Scooby-Doo underwear. Gavin laughed along while my father and I exchanged conspiratorial glances.

There was an amiable pause as the waitress came to take our order, and I glanced at the faces around the table to note that everyone was smiling.

Okay. Not too bad. Mom hadn't picked the *most* embarrassing story, and now the ice was broken. Maybe we'd get out of here unscathed after all.

"What about you? Any funny stories from when you were a kid?" my father asked before my mother could dive headlong into another Emma story.

This time Gavin did look taken aback, and a chill of

unease swept over me. "I had an . . . unusual childhood, so I'm not really sure I can think of anything funny off the top of my head."

"Unusual how?" my mother asked.

"Mom, if Gavin doesn't want to—"

Gavin squeezed my hand gently. "No, it's okay, Emma," he murmured and then cleared his throat. "Look, Mr. and Mrs. Bell, I grew up in what was practically a brothel, so most of the stories are inappropriate for table conversation."

My parents exchanged a telling glance, and then my mother poured herself more wine before managing a tight, insincere smile. "Well, that certainly is . . . untraditional."

"Explains your line of work, though," my dad muttered.

"Dad," I said, my tone a warning.

"What? Are we going to sit here and pretend we don't read the papers?" he demanded.

I blew out a frustrated sigh.

"No, it's okay," Gavin said. "I know the name is a little misleading and the press has been rough lately, but I don't run a brothel, sir. My business is completely moral and on the up and up. I pay my taxes, and we protect the women who work for us and pay them very well." Gavin said the words calmly but firmly, and my mother shifted in her chair.

And it wasn't just a line he was feeding them to placate the situation. Gavin and his brothers really did look after the women they employed. Stella, the girl who'd been caught with cocaine, had just completed a stay in rehab—all funded by their company. And not because they had to for publicity's sake, but just because they were good men.

My dad placed his elbows on the table, leaning closer, weighing Gavin's every word. "Paid very well, huh? And you think that makes it better?"

Gavin cleared his throat. "It's not prostitution, if that's what you're picturing. It's a glorified dating service."

This time, my mother spoke up. "That certainly is

good to hear. Now, I don't know about the rest of you, but I'm ready for some breadsticks."

As we dug in, things were awkward and quiet for a few minutes. But soon enough, my parents began peppering Gavin with questions about his business, his brothers, and the struggle he'd gone through to make something of himself. If Gavin was uncomfortable, he showed no signs of it. As the afternoon went on, my parents seemed more and more impressed with his fortitude and determination.

I wanted to cry with relief.

"I'm still dying to hear more stories about Emma, though," Gavin said when the long line of questions was over and we were almost through our meal.

I shot him a requisite glare, but in truth, I couldn't bring myself to be upset. Things were going even better than I could have imagined. As my mom launched into another story, I found myself glancing at Gavin from the corner of my eye, wondering how in the world I'd found a man so kind, confident, and wonderful.

When my mother's latest story—the time she caught

me practicing kissing on a pillow—wound down, Gavin turned to my father.

"Frank, do you think we could take a walk outside? Emma said you got a new car, and I'm dying to have a look."

It was literally the perfect thing to say.

Beaming, my dad practically leaped from his chair. "Sure thing. You're going to love this. The way this baby purrs, I'm telling you, there's nothing better."

Gavin followed him out the door while my mom slipped her credit card into the check folder the waitress had laid down.

"Thanks for everything, Mom," I said.

"Thank you for coming. I thought it was past time we met this man of yours, and now that we have? I can see that you were right. His business is certainly unconventional, but it's not like he's doing anything illegal. He's a good man. And good for you."

"You think?" My heart warmed at the soft words of approval.

Dirty Little Promise

"Based on the way you light up when he looks at you? I know it. It means a lot to a mother to see her child so happy."

"I am. I'm very happy," I said.

"Good. You deserve it, sweetie. You really do."

As I thought of the strife over the past year, I couldn't help but hope she was right.

Chapter Nineteen

Gavin

When Sunday came, Emma went on a shopping trip with her friend Bethany, leaving me to sit in my apartment and ruminate over yesterday's lunch.

In truth, I should have expected the questions about my past and the worries over my career. I'd been so focused on making Emma more comfortable, it hadn't even occurred to me, but in hindsight, I should have prepared myself.

Still, in spite of everything, it went even better than I could have hoped. Emma's parents were just like her—good listeners, respectful, interested. When we spoke, I could tell they really cared about whatever I was saying, small talk or no.

No bullshit. What you saw was what you got, and I liked that.

And more than anything? They were important to Emma. Which meant they were important to me now too.

When Frank and I had made our way out to the parking lot, he'd shown me his new car—a beautiful

Cadillac that Anne apparently didn't approve of. He made me peer under the hood and stroke the luxury seating, telling me twenty times or more that the seats could get either hot and cold at the touch of a button.

When he'd finished, he turned to me and said, "All right, now that I've had my fun, what did you really want to talk to me about?"

"How'd you know?"

He gave me a small smile. "I'm not an idiot. You could buy and sell me. You don't care about this car."

"It's a beautiful car," I said. "But you're right, I did want to talk to you about something else."

He nodded and crossed his arms over his chest.

"I love your daughter. Very much. So much that I want to spend the rest of my life with her, and I'd like your blessing."

Frank didn't appear surprised by this in the slightest. "You'll provide for her? I know it's old-fashioned, but it's important to me."

I nodded. "No matter what. She'll never want for anything."

"And you'll look after her? You'll never hurt her?"

"I could never, ever hurt her," I said sincerely.

"You'll love her even when it's hard?"

I understood his concerns only too well. Of course there would be hard times; there were in any marriage.

I nodded. "I'll love her until my last breath."

"Then you have my blessing, young man," he'd said. "Now, let's go inside before Anne orders another bottle of wine."

I'd grinned and followed him, but his words had been on my mind all day and night afterward, so much so that Emma had asked me what was wrong with me.

The fact that this was the one thing I couldn't stop thinking about, in spite of all the other things pressing on me? The lawsuit, the unresolved issues with Emma's safety, the press . . . the stress was tremendous, but all I could think about was getting on one knee and asking Emma to be my wife.

Dirty Little Promise

A fire lit inside me and I stood. Grabbing my jacket from the hook beside the door, I slipped it on and headed out onto the city streets. It was a chilly day, but luckily for me, the jeweler wasn't a far walk from my apartment. When I reached the store, I walked inside and made a beeline for the first display case of rings I could find.

"How can I help you today, sir?"

An older woman with auburn hair twisted into a knot smiled at me from behind the case, and I grinned back at her.

"I'm looking for an engagement ring for the most beautiful woman in the world."

"Oh, I'm so sorry to disappoint, but I'm already married, sir." She winked, and I chuckled.

"Could I see this one?" I pointed to a ring with a massive round diamond nestled in the center of a halo of smaller diamonds. The band was platinum, and as I took it in my hand, I held it out, trying to imagine it on Emma's slender finger.

I shook my head. "I don't think that one's quite

right."

The saleswoman took it back, then reached for a new selection. "How about this one?"

This was a more traditional ring. A five-carat diamond sat in the center of a cluster of diamonds that lined the entire band. It was paired with a matching wedding ring with an equal number of glittering stones. As I looked at the shimmering confection of a ring, it practically blinded me, but I knew this, too, wasn't right for Emma.

I frowned and shook my head. "Not that one either."

The woman took the ring back and placed it inside the case again. "Maybe it would help if we had a price point?" she asked carefully.

I shook my head. "Price is no object."

She rose her eyebrows. "All right then, what about this?"

She moved to another case and took out another ring, heavier than the others when she placed it in the center of my palm. The stone must have been at least ten karats, and it was flawless in every light. On either side of the rock sat two smaller, but equally impressive diamonds, and underneath was a diamond-encrusted band that hugged each of the cushion-cut stones.

"This is stunning." I held the ring out, examining it in the light as I tried to picture the look on Emma's face when she saw it. It was truly the most beautiful ring I'd ever laid eyes on, but it still wasn't quite right. Not for Emma. Shaking my head, I handed the ring back to the woman.

She took it, then tilted her head to the side. "Tell me a little bit about your fiancée, maybe?"

My fiancée. I liked the sound of that.

"She's perfect. Easy to be around, and just as beautiful in no makeup and jeans as she is in a ball gown. She's comfortable everywhere, but she likes being home the best. She's refurbishing her grandmother's old brownstone herself, and she loves to read. She's the kind of girl who'd rather sit by the pool than go on a spa retreat." I smiled, thinking about her in her polka-dot bikini.

The woman's eyes softened and she nodded thoughtfully. "So, she appreciates the simple things in life."

"She does."

"I know just the ring." She disappeared for a moment and then approached me with a red crushed-velvet box.

Snapping it open, I found a single solitaire inside set on a classic band. The diamond was flawless, a round stone with brilliant light pouring from every angle. It was simple and perfect, just like Emma. It would enhance the beauty of her trim little hand instead of overpowering it.

But best of all? It would make her smile when she looked at it. I knew it in my gut.

"This is perfect," I said.

"I thought so. Would you like to know the price?"

"That's not necessary. I'll take this one."

I followed her to the cash register and settled the bill, then tucked the tiny box in my pocket before making my way back onto the street, thinking again of Emma's parents. I wondered if she would want them there when I proposed, and tried to imagine what sort of proposal she would want.

Probably nothing too glitzy or over the top. There would be no skywriting, no flash mob with signs. Just a few candles and the two of us.

Classic, just like the ring and just like Emma.

As the gears in my mind worked, I felt my phone vibrate and I grabbed it, not bothering to look at the number before pressing the phone to my ear.

"Hello?" I said.

"Mr. Kingsley, it's Aaron Deacon."

My lawyer.

"Mr. Deacon, hello. What's going on?"

"I'm reviewing your case and was wondering if you'd had any more time to consider our plan of action. Have you spoken with your business partners?"

I cleared my throat. "No. I haven't."

"I've been doing some case research, and it's my job to tell you I think it's prudent that you settle out of court at this juncture. I just don't see this going away."

I pursed my lips. "Go on."

"I looked into the plaintiffs' background to see if they could sustain such an extended trial, and it would appear that they were recently the victors in another lawsuit against a pharmaceutical company—"

"Whom they were suing on Ashley's behalf," I said, finishing for him.

"Yes. The settlement was substantial, and I think they'll be prepared to put the screws to you if push comes to shove. To have something like this in the papers over the course of weeks? Very bad for business."

"And how much would you suggest I settle for?"

"Five million. It's a lot less than what they're asking, but like I said, they only want the money."

I pinched my nose and let out a long breath. "Right."

"Like I said, I felt obligated to tell you. Discuss it with your family and your business partners, and then get back to me as soon as you can. We're running out of time here."

"Okay, I will." I ended the call, then scrolled over to Quinn's number, staring at it for a long moment before stuffing my phone back in my pocket.

A settlement that large would crush the company, not just financially but ethically. Even as I rolled the issue over and over in my mind, I couldn't get past the idea that a settlement would make things look exactly as they weren't—that Ashley's parents had cared about her, and that I was the source of her pain.

In all the time I'd known her, all I had ever done was try to make her life better, to make her happy. There was evidence of that in all my memories, all the times I'd sat by her hospital bed.

Which meant, no matter what happened, a jury should be able to see that too.

I couldn't cut and run. No, I had to find a way to tell Quinn and Cooper the truth.

The ring burned like a brand in my pocket, and I

swallowed hard.

And Emma too.

Chapter Twenty

Emma

I spent the next week alternating between work and Gavin's place. Or, more specifically, Gavin's bed.

In the days after our lunch with my parents, I could tell there was still something weighing on his mind, but aside from that, things were good between us.

We were finally growing together, just like any normal couple would. Making memories and creating traditions.

We'd lie in bed together, naked and panting, and then we'd flip on the television and watch shows about house renovations or documentaries about food production in faraway places. It didn't matter the topic; Gavin found a way to make everything interesting.

As I lay in his arms each night, I could feel myself sinking deeper, wishing I could stay there forever and always.

Of course, it wasn't all roses. Some nights I still woke up, my heart pounding from a nightmare about that car bearing down on me, or about the bloody, pulpy mess left on my porch. There were little reminders of the threat everywhere.

The fact that I could no longer drive or take the bus, and still had to have the driver take me wherever I wanted to go.

The police officer stationed outside the library whenever I was at work.

The memory of that bloody bag every time I passed my stoop.

Today had been one of the days where I couldn't just forget about it all. Bethany had taken a personal day, and the library had closed early due to a major leak in one of the bathrooms, leaving me all alone with my thoughts. By the time afternoon rolled around, I didn't hesitate before clicking the ANSWER button on my cell phone when it rang.

"Hi, Mom."

"Emma, honey." My mom's sugary tones wafted over the receiver, making me relax into my chair at the comforting sound of her voice. "I was just wondering what you were up to tonight?"

Funny you should ask. I was planning on wallowing in fear while I waited for my boyfriend to get home.

"Nothing. Why, is everything okay?" I asked.

"Fine, fine. I was just hoping you could come up for a visit. I know it's a little bit of a drive, but I was thinking we could go to the tea house for dinner, and you could spend the night."

I glanced at the clock. In order to meet Mom in time for dinner, I'd have to leave pretty much as soon as I locked up for the day. But Gavin was working late tonight anyway, and I wasn't looking forward to my evening alone.

"That sounds great, Mom, but can I ask . . . I mean, I just saw you last weekend. Are you sure everything is fine?"

"I promise, everything is great. I just want to see my girl."

I breathed a hesitant sigh of relief. Sometimes a little alone time with Mom was the best remedy.

"Well, then, how can I refuse? I'll see you in a couple

of hours."

Quickly, I shot a text to Gavin and then to my driver before gathering my things and shoving them into my oversized work bag. My slacks and sweater would have to be good enough for the tea room, though I knew my mother would insist I try to squeeze into one of my old dresses from high school that still hung in my closet at their house.

No, thank you.

When my car arrived, I jogged down the steps and ducked inside, joining my driver in the front seat and changing the radio to my favorite station.

"Good afternoon, Emma," Felix said with a grin.

"Hey, Felix. Did you get the directions okay?"

He gave me a thumbs-up and we sped onto the street. Luckily, we'd gotten out before the worst of the rush-hour traffic. Still, I felt bad about dragging Felix so far away on such short notice.

Digging my phone from my pocket, I pinged a text to Gavin.

Can you give Felix a tip or a bonus or something from me? I'll give you the money when I get home.

Gavin replied in a matter of seconds.

Already done, but I'm not taking money from you. Have a great time.

Frowning, but knowing better than to argue, I shoved my phone back in my pocket and concentrated on the road ahead.

My mom could say it was nothing but a casual visit, but so many impromptu trips in a row had me slightly on edge. I just hoped, if my suspicions were right, that it didn't have anything to do with Gavin. She'd admitted she misjudged him, after all. What else was there to say on the subject?

Two hours later, Felix pulled into my parents' driveway and escorted me to the door. I rang the doorbell, then insisted he head back to the car before my mother opened the door with a wide grin.

"Hey, Mom." I smiled back. "Where's Daddy?"

"Bowling. I thought it'd be nice to have a girls'

night."

"You're right; it is. Sorry, but I didn't have a dress on me for the tea room."

"Well, you could always—"

"I'm not going to try on my old dresses," I said quickly. "Come on, let's go."

Under Felix's watchful gaze, I headed to my mother's car and got inside, and when we pulled out onto the main road, he was directly behind us.

"Should I be nervous about the man in the black car following us?"

"Oh." I let out a nervous laugh, heat rushing to my face. "No, that's my driver, Felix. He's supposed to look after me, that's all."

My mother raised her eyebrows. "Gavin's orders, I'm guessing?"

"You got it." I adjusted my collar. "I know it's a little silly."

"But sweet too. He's looking out for you."

A few minutes later, my mother pulled in front of an old Victorian building. After parking, we made our way to the wrought-iron door.

"Your grandmother loved this place," Mom cooed as she always did when we walked inside and saw the polished wood floors and the vintage chandeliers. A girl in a white shirt and bow tie approached us and led us to a table already laden with scones, clotted cream, and tea cookies.

As ever, my mother ordered us one pot of Earl Grey and another of jasmine tea before tucking into her scone.

For a while, we chatted easily—me discussing the library's latest events and acquisitions, and her talking about the latest news on the retired-teacher circuit. The tea arrived, and we each poured a cup of our preferred favorite, Earl Grey. The jasmine, though neither of us would say it, was for my grandmother. It would sit between us untouched, but the scent of it comforted us both and made it feel like she was still here with us in some way.

"So, tell me more about this boy," my mom finally

said.

I giggled without warning. "I hardly think Gavin's a boy, Mom. He's thirty-four years old."

She smiled. "I suppose that's true."

The truth was, it didn't matter his age. Gavin was all man.

"I'm actually more curious to hear your thoughts," I admitted. "Now that you've met him, what do you think?"

"I think he's a good man. He's smart. Driven. A good businessperson. And he obviously cares for you."

"But?" I raised my eyebrows.

"But . . . I wonder if you think he'll be there for you. Sometimes, in the beginning, it's hard to tell things like that. And a man with so many interests, so much money, can can he be counted on in good times and bad?"

"I think so," I said, suddenly filled with apprehension.

My mother shook her head. "That's not good enough, sweets."

"Where is this coming from?" I asked, my brow furrowed.

She let out a deep breath. "Did you ever wonder why your parents were so much older than everyone else's?"

My frown deepened. My mother had been forty when I was born. "Truthfully? I guessed I was an accident. Not in a bad way, but like a surprise."

My mother tilted her head to the side, looking at me with a new kind of softness in her eyes. Slowly, she shook her head. "No, not at all. I never told you everything, really. That's the way of it with mothers. We don't want to burden our children with our own pain, but maybe it's time I told you the whole story."

A pause lingered in the air, and she took a sip of her tea before spreading her hands wide on the frilly tablecloth.

"Your father and I married when we were eighteen. We were stupid and in love, and back then, college wasn't as important as it is today. We worked our menial jobs, and your father supported me while I went back to school to become a teacher."

I nodded. "I know."

"But what you don't know is, hard as all that was, we were struggling with something else. See, the thing we wanted most of all was a baby. We tried and tried. I had five miscarriages in a ten-year period. And then, well, when we turned thirty, we decided it was time to stop trying. I tried to move on. Tried to feel fulfilled with my job and my life as it was. After all, lots of people choose not to have children, right?"

Her sad smile broke my heart as she continued. "But I got depressed. Not the blues, or feeling low, but the kind of depression where you can't get out of bed or think of a reason to bother brushing your hair."

"Oh, Mom," I whispered, taking her hand in mine, and she rolled her thumb absently over the back of it.

"And you know what? Your father was my rock. He stood with me that year, never once wavering. Not when I lost my job because of it, not when I broke down or took it out on him. He stayed and we got through it. Eventually, we found our happiness together." Her lips trembled into a smile. "So, when I was forty and got pregnant with you? You were our miracle, Emma. Never,

ever an accident. But the important part of this particular story is, if it never happened? If we'd never been blessed with having you? That strife, those dark times, they let me know in my heart that I had the right man."

"That's beautiful," I said, tears pricking my eyes.

She shook her head. "It's what it should be. So, my question to you is this, my sweet daughter. Whatever life throws at you—the pain and the heartache and the joys—is this the person you want by your side?"

My answer came to me without hesitation. "He's the one, Mom. I know it."

I only hoped he felt the same.

Chapter Twenty-One

Gavin

"We've got a problem," Quinn barked, shoving through the door as he let himself inside my office.

For fuck's sake. I pushed away from my laptop, readying myself for the latest catastrophe. "What now?"

We'd had a string of problems to sort through lately, and I'd hoped our troubles were over. Maybe it was all part of being a Kingsley. Shit, maybe we were cursed.

Quinn released a tired groan and dropped into the leather chair opposite me. He was two years older than me, but somehow managed to seem both older and younger at once. He was experienced and wise, and when he spoke, men listened. But at the same time, he'd never really been in a relationship, had never even come close to settling down, so he still maintained that sort of bachelor's immaturity.

"Cooper's gone again."

Jesus. I pinched the bridge of my nose, suddenly tired. Cooper had taken off for a while, trying to find himself, whatever that meant. But he'd come back, still not sure where he was going to settle. I knew he'd be moving and soon, but his disappearing act was getting old. I was used to predictability, and this was anything but business as usual.

"One of us needs to go after him, and I think it should be you, for obvious reasons."

"Me?" I let out a grunt of surprise. Quinn's reasons were far from obvious to me.

"Yes. You."

"I have no patience for his drama. I got the girl. End of story. He needs to man up."

Honestly, I thought we'd covered all this, thought we'd worked through this that evening at Quinn's when Emma disappeared into the library to let him down easy. Of course, I should have known it would never be that simple. Real life was often messy—I knew that better than anyone.

"How would you feel if the tables were turned? If Cooper was with Emma right now, and you were the odd man out?"

Strange. That was a notion I'd never even considered.

"I sure as hell wouldn't be off somewhere hiding, licking my wounds." I scoffed. "I'd be here—where I'm needed—working."

"Yes, you would. But you'd be a surly son of bitch and a nightmare to deal with. And we both know it."

There was no arguing with Quinn. Plus, there was a tiny chance that he might be right. Which I hated.

"My point is that everyone handles things differently. If you could put yourself in his shoes for just a moment, you'd understand how incredibly difficult it must be for him to see you and Emma together. And asking him to stay with her while you were out of town?" Quinn made a low noise of disapproval in his throat and shook his head. "That was fucked up, bro."

Then why did you fucking suggest it, asshole? Anger bubbled up inside me, but it was clear this was not the time to argue.

Now I was the one releasing a frustrated sigh. "Fine. I'll go after him. Where is he?"

"New York."

• • •

Pleased that I was able to get the jet on short notice, I'd headed to New York for the evening. Emma had gone to visit her parents' home for the night a couple of hours away, which meant I didn't have to worry about leaving her unattended. I had a nagging feeling that the mess she'd found herself in wasn't quite over yet. But I'd have to deal with that later.

Quinn had told me that Cooper had checked himself into the swanky Lancaster hotel in the heart of the city. When I got to reception and learned he'd booked himself the presidential suite—on the company credit card—my blood pressure skyrocketed, but I promised myself I wouldn't deck the son of a bitch upon entry.

When I knocked, Cooper took his time, the door only finally opening several minutes later. He was dressed in a pair of gray sweatpants, the cashmere ones that Quinn had gotten him the Christmas before, and a wrinkled black T-shirt. He hadn't shaved in days, his hair was a mess, and if I didn't know better, I'd swear he'd opted out of showering these past few days. *Nice*.

"You look like shit." I pushed past him, letting myself inside.

"Hello, brother dearest."

Noting his monotone voice, I wondered if he'd fought Quinn over the idea of my visit. Probably.

"Get dressed," I said. "We're going to dinner."

Cooper dropped onto the plush sofa. "No thanks. I'd rather stay in."

This was going well. My gaze scanned the suite, zeroing in on a glass bar cart at the far end of the living area. The crystal decanter of bourbon was calling to me.

Pouring myself a measure, I ignored his pointed stare and the anger I could feel rolling off him in waves.

"You just can't handle not calling the shots, can you, Gavin?" he taunted.

I blew out a frustrated sigh and took a sip of my drink, appreciating its fiery burn. "I've been taking care of you since we were kids, Cooper. You really need me to play that role again?"

"Nope. Not even a fucking little bit. I just wanted a moment to myself, which is apparently a concept too great for you and Quinn to grasp."

Rolling my eyes, I refilled my glass and made my way to the sofa, sinking into the seat beside him. "So . . ." I paused, hoping he'd fill in the blank and make this a little easier on me.

"That's your attempt at small talk? You suck at this, by the way."

"Look, I'm sorry, okay? You practically pushed me toward Emma, and you were right. She's perfect. And she means the world to me, Coop. I still don't think I actually deserve her, but . . . fuck. She's it for me."

"I need a fucking drink," he muttered, rising to his feet. Once he'd poured himself a glass of bourbon, he joined me on the couch again.

I waited while he took a long swallow.

"I get it," he said finally, his voice raw.

Releasing a slow exhale, I tried to put myself in his shoes. "I do too. If you'd been the one to . . ." I couldn't even let myself go there. If Cooper had ended up with Emma? It wasn't a scenario I could even let myself imagine. I'd be destroyed.

"Thanks for acknowledging that. And for what it's worth, I am sorry about the way she found out about Ashley."

I took another sip of my drink, waiting for him to continue.

"Honestly, I thought you'd told her. Figured you guys had covered exes and all that. But when I mentioned Ashley's name, Emma's blank stare immediately told me I was wrong. I tried to backpedal, but you know Emma. She loves a good mystery."

I'd been meaning to tell Emma, knew I had to at some point. I'd just thought I had more time. It wasn't all his fault.

"You're my brother, and I love you, Coop. I forgive you for telling Emma about Ashley."

He nodded. "And I forgive you for getting the girl. In the back of my mind, I kind of always knew it would go that way."

I gave him a sad smile. The older brother in me still needed to look out for him. "So, we're all good?"

"Yeah. Let's get drunk."

He crossed the room to grab the ice bucket and bourbon while I reached for the room service menu.

"What's good here?" I asked, figuring he'd probably been eating most of his meals in.

"The bison burger and the omelet are the only things I've had."

I nodded as I dialed, and ordered us a couple of burgers and another bottle of bourbon.

When our food arrived a short time later, we dug in, falling into easy conversation, just like old times. Cooper clicked on the TV, and we watched the sports highlights over dinner.

"There's more I need to tell you," I said, stacking our dinner dishes on the cart the attendant had left.

"So, tell me. We've already ripped off the bandage, don't you think?"

He was right. We were each two glasses of bourbon in, and I was feeling loose.

Letting out a heavy sigh, I decided to tell him the bad news first. "There's a lawsuit against me. Ashley's parents are suing for wrongful death. Ten million dollars. I'm the only defendant, so it shouldn't affect the company." At least, I'd do everything within my control to make sure it didn't.

Cooper rose to his feet. "That's bullshit. Does Quinn know?"

"Not yet."

"We need to tell him. He'd agree with me that we need to use every tool in our arsenal to fight this. You're not facing his alone. The best lawyer, whatever we have to do. A counter lawsuit if we have to—her parents knew about her pill problem and did nothing. You, on the other hand, tried to help her."

His response was unexpected and warmed my chest. I'd figured I'd go this alone from beginning to end. Figured I might even have to step down from my position at Forbidden Desires, because the last thing we needed was more bad press.

"You're the first person I've told, but yes, I'll tell him," I added. "Thank you. This was more support than I expected."

Cooper offered me a sad smile as he lowered himself to his seat again. "I'm just sorry you have to relive it. That is seriously fucked up."

It wasn't something I wanted to do, that was for sure. But part of being an adult was dealing with all the shit you'd rather pretend didn't exist.

And from Ashley's parents' standpoint? They had lost their daughter. Nothing would bring her back, but they weren't going to just let her go and move on without a fight.

"There's something else." I added more bourbon to my glass, even though it wasn't quite empty. Something told me I was going to need it. "I've decided to propose to Emma."

Cooper swallowed hard, his eyes closing for a moment. "Congratulations."

A heavy silence that hadn't been there before settled between us. I held my tongue, knowing he needed a minute to process this latest news.

When he reopened his eyes, he said, "Tell her about the lawsuit first."

How did we get here? My little brother was now giving me relationship advice. I didn't respond.

"If you haven't bought a ring yet, I have some advice. Even though you didn't ask." He grinned. "Don't get her some big, gaudy diamond. She wouldn't want that."

I nodded, only slightly annoyed that he knew her so well. "She's a simple girl, I agree."

Damn. Look at us—sharing our feelings and shit. Quinn would be so proud.

"I need to take a piss," he said, rising to his feet.

Our conversation was over. But we'd both survived, so there was that.

When Cooper returned, he was dressed in a pair of dark jeans and a black button-down shirt. His hair was styled and his eyes were alight with mischief.

"I need to go out and get laid. Be my wingman?" he said.

It wasn't a good idea. We were both drunk, and it was almost midnight. But I knew first-hand the raw hunger he was probably experiencing. He needed something to control, needed to possess and own someone in all the ways he'd never command Emma. My heart broke a little for him just then.

"Always." I rose to my feet, following him toward the door.

As we waited for the elevator, I couldn't help but look him over. We'd shared a lot tonight, and I felt closer because of it. Still slightly uneasy, but closer nonetheless.

"Can I ask you one more thing?" I asked as the elevator doors opened.

"'Course," he said over his shoulder as I followed him inside.

Cooper's green eyes met mine. For a second, it was too intense, and I almost backed out on asking him. Almost.

"Do you still love her?"

"Always," he said, mirroring my comment from before. He didn't hesitate. Didn't so much as blink.

A rock settled in the pit of my stomach as we descended, and suddenly all that bourbon seemed like a terrible idea.

It was a long and silent ride to the lobby. As the elevator doors opened, I was struck by the realization that if I ever fucked up again, Cooper would have her, and there'd be nothing I could do.

Chapter Twenty-Two

Emma

Reunited again at Gavin's place, we wasted little time before falling into bed together.

"So, now that we've caught up a little, tell me . . . was it bad?" I asked after we'd lain in each other's arms for an hour, recovering from our second round of lovemaking.

"The sex? Never." Gavin grinned down at me.

I frowned, then shook my head. "Your trip. You haven't said a word about it."

"Oh." Gavin took a deep breath. "I don't want you worrying about that."

"We said no secrets," I reminded him.

His soulful eyes stared into mine, and he let out a gentle sigh. "We did. The trip wasn't bad, but it wasn't ideal. Cooper . . . I'd rather not tell you how he's doing. I know he needs the time away, though."

So, it's as bad as I feared.

"That must be hard on you," I said softly, rubbing

Gavin's bicep, and he flexed beneath my touch.

"A little. It's hard to know I was the cause of all this, you know? I never meant for this to happen."

"We were the cause," I reminded him gently, refusing to let myself off the hook. "And I didn't mean for it to happen either." I pursed my lips. "It's one of those things that will take time, I think."

"I know you're right." He kissed my forehead. "As usual."

I offered him a soft smile, and another silence passed between us before he sat up in bed.

"All right, what do you want to do today?"

"This?" I asked, turning over and letting the sheets fall away from me so he could see my naked body. He surveyed me with hooded eyes, studying my breasts, the space between my thighs, but then he shook his head.

"You make a tempting argument. But are you sure there's nothing you want to do? I don't want to keep you chained to the bed all day."

"Yes, because I'd hate that."

Dirty Little Promise 323

He smirked at me. "Come here, woman. While you think about what you'd like to do today, there's something I want to tell you."

I wondered if it was something about his visit with Cooper, but Gavin stayed quiet for a few more seconds, leaving me in suspense.

"What is it, baby?" I asked him, bringing my palm to his stubbled cheek.

He was quiet for a second, his eyes locked on mine. "I'm . . . crazy fucking in love with you," he finally murmured.

"Gavin." I sighed, totally taken by surprise.

I'd waited so long to hear those words from him, and this declaration—so bold and sure—I could almost have laughed if I weren't so caught up in the moment. Gavin didn't do anything halfway. He was always brave and confident, and how he expressed his love was no different.

"I love you too, a million billion," I whispered, pressing my lips to his.

"Right back at you, baby." He kissed my lips softly as we lingered together in a state of bliss.

After we'd cuddled and kissed and exchanged a few more I-love-yous, which felt so natural and right, Gavin was back to grinning down at me.

"Have you thought of anything you'd like to do today?" he asked again.

"I wouldn't mind going shopping at the fancy organic market you turned me on to. I'd love to make you my grandma's homemade chicken potpie. It has this flaky puff-pastry crust that's to die for."

"Sounds great."

I sat up in bed. "The only thing is, all my clean clothes are back at my place."

"Then we'll go there, and I'll watch you try on dresses." Gavin shrugged. "Easy."

"Okay." I grinned, then quickly slipped into a sweatshirt and worn jeans before following him down to the car.

We pulled onto my street with its rows of little

brownstones, all uniform and perfect in a row—

All except mine, which had a giant hole where the door should have been.

The planters outside were cracked, as if someone had taken a mallet to them, and the splintered wood from the door was scattered on the steps like shrapnel after an explosion.

"Oh my God," I whispered, the familiar feeling of cold, bitter violation coiling through me.

"Fuck." Gavin snarled, his whole body tensing. "Stay in the car," he warned me when we'd finally parked.

But I couldn't. How could I just sit here and wait? I had to see for myself what this person—what *Nathan*—had done to my grandmother's house.

I waited until Gavin got out of the car and disappeared into the brownstone to follow him, stepping numbly into the place that had once been my home.

And the second I saw it? It was even worse than I'd imagined.

The hardwood floors, original to the old building, were gouged and carved up. The moldings I'd so carefully painted were wrenched from the walls. All my work, my hours of devotion to make this place just like my grandmother's house had been, was ruined.

My heart pounded as I pulled my cell phone from my pocket, dialing the numbers without thinking. When the police dispatcher answered, I gave her all the information calmly and quietly, then waited while she gave me instructions.

This was a crime scene now. Soon, I'd hear sirens roaring down the street, and would be asked to answer even more questions. But I couldn't worry about that now.

All I could think was, what kind of person would do such a thing?

And what would they have done if they'd come here to find me home, maybe asleep in my bed?

I wrapped my arms around myself and shivered, thinking of the way Nathan had thrown me into dressers and desks. The way he'd knocked my head against walls.

Dirty Little Promise

How badly he'd hurt me.

It wasn't impossible to think he'd reached the tipping point. That he might have taken his mallet to my skull too.

A creaking on the stairs let me know that Gavin was approaching. I looked up at him, trying to keep my face impassive as his gaze met mine. If he was surprised to see me there, he didn't show it. In fact, he showed nothing but raw fury.

I swayed on my feet as I tried to think clearly. "I think he'll really kill me, Gavin. Nathan will stop at nothing." I motioned around the room. "If this doesn't prove it, I don't know what would."

He shook his head. "It wasn't Nathan."

"What?"

"It wasn't Nathan," he insisted, his jaw clenched. "Come with me upstairs."

I followed him wordlessly, only stopping short for a moment when I noticed the ocean of feathers in my hall. As I opened the door to my bedroom, however, I realized exactly what had happened. Whoever had done this had taken a knife to my down comforter and pillows, scattering a million feathers over the whole room. I repressed a shiver at the sheer violence of it.

"Here." Gavin pointed to the wide mirror over my dresser. In my favorite red lipstick, someone had written *Die, Bitch* in spiky, jagged cursive.

"Creative," I said in a deadpan voice, still trying to process what had happened here.

"No. Not that." He shook his head. "The writing. I recognize it."

I blinked.

"This was Sonja," he muttered, raking a hand over his face. "Sonja has been the one doing this. You said the car that hit you was red? Sonja drives a red car."

And Sonja had been trying to seduce him for weeks, only to be shot down.

A woman scorned . . .

The revelation was so shocking, I could barely keep up.

"So, what do we do?" I asked.

"We tell the police so they can arrest her."

As he finished speaking, the sound of approaching sirens grew until they echoed around us.

When the police arrived, we told them everything. And just as easily as Gavin had said, Sonja was taken in for questioning.

Within an hour, she'd broken down and told the whole story of what she'd done. How she'd left the bloody mess on my doorstep. How she'd tried to kill me in the street that day. How she'd tried again last night, and lost her mind when I wasn't there.

It was hard to hear it all, to know someone could harbor so much malice against me, but when she was taken into custody and we were free to go, I headed home with a renewed sense of freedom.

No more wondering or second-guessing. I was finally safe.

Still, as we sailed down the road, I couldn't help but notice Gavin's mood. Tension remained in his jaw and his shoulders, and as we made our way closer to his apartment, it only seemed to get worse.

"What's going on?" I asked.

"Nothing," he said, clearly lying.

"Pull over."

Gavin did as I asked with a sigh.

When we were on the side of the road, a steady stream of cars whizzing past, I twisted in my seat to face Gavin.

"What's going on?" I repeated. "I thought you'd be relieved that they caught Sonja. Everything is going to be okay now."

"I'm struggling with the fact that, yet again, the trouble in your life was due to me," he said, his face a mask of guilt. "Everything bad that's happened to you is because you're with me."

"Not true," I shot back angrily, gripping his arm tight. "Nathan was before I ever knew you, and this—"

"This could have ended so much worse, Emma.

You're the fucking sun, and I'm nothing but a dark cloud blotting out your light."

"Gavin, you *are* the light," I said, pleading with him now, hating the sadness in his eyes. "Please, it's over now. It's only blue skies ahead for us. I love you."

"I love you too, baby. But there's something else," he said, finally meeting my gaze. "I know we said no secrets, but I haven't been completely honest with you. I thought with everything with Sonja . . . well, I didn't think it was a good time. Now that it's over, though, I want you to know."

I took a steadying breath, preparing myself for whatever came next. "Tell me."

"Ashley's family is suing me for ten million dollars. It will ruin me personally and the company if I lose. My attorney wants me to settle out of court, but I can't."

For the next fifteen minutes, the whole story poured out. How he'd wanted to tell me, how he'd told Cooper, what Ashley's family had been like when she needed them.

He left out no detail, and when he was done, he looked up at me again, his eyes pleading for forgiveness. "I know I should have told you. I'm sorry, but damn it, it's all too much."

I shook my head. "Don't worry about that now. What's done is done, but from this moment forward, there are no secrets between us. No matter what."

He nodded. "But what about everything else?"

"What about it?" I shrugged. "We're strong. Win or lose, we'll get through this. We just have to make sure we do it together."

Gavin had stood by me through the worst of times, and now, I would do the same.

"Come on. Let's go to the store. I think we need that comfort food now more than ever," I told him.

Chapter Twenty-Three

Emma

Another week came and went as Gavin and I pushed through what we hoped would be the worst of his case. We looked for receipts, and talked to people who might be willing to testify. And, finally, Gavin told Quinn everything about the case.

It was hard for Gavin, going back through all the trials and tribulations of his time with the woman he'd loved. Although I'd expected to feel jealous or possessive, the more I learned about Ashley, the sadder I felt for both of them.

Meanwhile, I was dealing with the issues of Sonja's upcoming sentencing. Since she'd confessed to everything, there would be no trial. She was facing three years in prison for aggravated assault.

I still couldn't bring myself to go back to the brownstone. Despite it all, I was surprised I didn't feel like the world was coming undone around me. Whenever I thought of my ruined house or my wasted effort, I felt so bitter that I wanted to scream and break down. But I didn't.

And that was all because of Gavin.

No matter how bad things got, I could look to him or tell him about it, confident in the knowledge he was sharing the load with me. I wasn't alone.

Day after day, I would look at him, either while helping him through his case or while telling him about my own heartache, and I'd find myself thinking of my conversation with my mother. He was the one for me—I knew it in my heart. We were building a foundation for something real. Something lasting.

The only question was whether he felt the same way.

I wanted to ask. My insecurities made me wonder what might happen next, but I kept my thoughts to myself. Gavin had enough to deal with without me getting all weird on him.

Instead, I focused on the library, hoping work would take my mind off the brownstone, the case, and my own concerns. When Friday came, I was working late building a book tree in the children's section. The bell rang at the door and I turned, ready to tell the visitor the library was closed, and I caught sight of Gavin.

He was wearing the charcoal suit I loved best, the same one he'd been wearing the day I walked into his office for the first time. At the sight at him, I felt my heart bubble over with warmth, and I grinned.

"Come to help with this book tree? I can't get to all the branches."

He shook his head as he pushed his hands into his pockets. "Not today. We have plans."

"We do?"

He nodded. "We do. Now, come on or we'll be late."

I gave my book tree a last glance, then followed him to the door and out into the street, golden with the warm glow of sunset. His limo wasn't there, but he led me to his car and helped me inside before climbing behind the wheel.

"Where's Ben?"

"Gave him the night off. I wanted it to just be the two of us." He stuck the key in the ignition, but before he twisted it, he turned in his seat and handed me a gift-wrapped rectangle.

"What's this?" I asked.

"Open it."

I peeled away the shiny white paper to reveal a beautiful leather-bound copy of the complete works of Jane Austen.

"How did you—"

"When we were watching *Sense and Sensibility*. You mentioned you didn't have physical copies."

"Thank you." I ran my fingers over the embossed title, tears threatening my eyes.

"Open it," he said again.

I opened the cover of the book to find the word *Will* scrawled in Gavin's untidy writing.

"It's already got the beginnings of an inscription here for someone named Will." I frowned as I glanced at him, puzzled.

"Does it? Weird."

Gavin started the car and pulled out onto the street while I examined the book. Before long, he pulled up to a shady patch of woods and I looked around, taking in the bluff that overlooked the city.

"This is—" I didn't finish. He knew what I was going to say.

It was the place where we'd touched for the first time. It had been the first time he'd ever let me get close to him, and it was a night I thought about often. The night I considered the true start of it all.

Silently, he got out of the car and opened the trunk to pull out another wrapped package. Sliding back into the driver's seat, he handed it to me.

I didn't need instruction this time. I ripped the paper away to find a copy of *Sighs, Cries, and Broken Things*, one of the books from the poetry reading we'd gone to together.

Grinning, I looked up at him. "Did you read this?"

"I was hoping we could read more of it together. But right now? All I want you to do is open it."

I did, and on a blank page inside the cover was written the word *You*. Nothing else.

My heart beat a little faster as I began to put two and two together, but I couldn't get ahead of myself. I just needed to be here, in the moment with him. To enjoy whatever was happening and not expect anything more than that.

Still, I held my breath as we pulled back onto the street, the radio turned down low as we drove past a row of brownstones and stopped at one with a construction sign in front of it. I blinked.

"This is my house," I said.

"It is. Come on."

He got out of the car and opened my door for me, then led me up to the stoop and unlocked the beautiful new turn-of-the-century door. We stepped inside the little foyer where the floors were still scratched and gouged, but I could tell work was being done here.

"What's all this?" I asked.

"I'm having your place renovated. I know how much it means to you."

As happy as this made me, my heart sank a little.

Gavin wasn't asking me to marry him after all. It was just this beautiful, wonderful surprise.

"Thank you," I whispered.

"But that's not why we're here."

I looked up at him. "It's not?"

He shook his head, then pulled a gift-wrapped book from my bookshelf. I tore the paper away and opened the front cover, this time finding the word *Marry* written inside.

I couldn't stop the tears from welling in my eyes. "Oh my God."

Gavin grinned and backed away. "We're not done yet, love. Come on."

Overwhelmed, I followed him back to the car, my whole body trembling.

When we got to his apartment, I followed him to his apartment without a word, waiting for the final surprise. When we got there, though, my heart practically stopped.

Candles flickered from every surface, including the

floor strewn with rose petals. Gavin led me through the beautiful scene he'd created for me to his bedroom where a book was waiting, wrapped in glossy white paper.

My hands shaking, I pulled the paper away to find a leather-bound journal. Its pages were blank, save for the first one where the word *Me* was written.

"I thought the journal could be our fresh start. Some pages to fill with our story."

I bit my lower lip as tears sprang to my eyes again. When Gavin slowly sank to one knee in front of me, the tears fell fresh and strong.

"Gavin," I said, barely able to choke out the word.

"Sweet Emma, when I met you, I was broken." He stroked my knuckles with his fingertips. "But you saw past all that; you accepted me and all my flaws. You challenged me to be a better man, and for that I owe you immensely. I love you with all my heart, and I can't imagine growing old with anyone else. You're the one I want. Just you."

I swallowed hard, nodding along as tears rolled down my cheeks. "I love you too, so much."

"The story of our love is only beginning. It's time to write our own happy ending."

Gavin swallowed, growing more emotional than I'd ever seen him. He reached into his pocket, withdrawing a little square box. When he opened it and pulled out the most exquisite ring, my heart almost stopped. It was old-fashioned and simple, but gorgeous. Absolutely perfect.

I couldn't believe this was happening.

"Marry me, pet?"

I drew a deep, shuddering breath. "Yes, Gavin, yes. I will marry you."

I held out my hand and he slid the ring on easily, kissing my fingers when he was done.

But I wanted more than that. So much more.

Dropping to my knees in front of him, I grabbed his face and crushed my lips to his, wanting him to feel how much I appreciated everything he'd done, all the thought he'd clearly put into every moment of this night. There was no flash or public fanfare. Instead, it was exactly how it was supposed to be—just us. Private and intimate.

"I love you so much," he murmured.

"A million billion," I told him.

I think he felt my appreciation because he led me to the bed and I fell on top of the covers, barely breathing as he pulled away my clothes. In the glow of the candlelight, I lay back and watched as he shrugged off his jacket and dragged his shirt over his head, revealing the chiseled stone of his abs. He unbuckled his belt and let his pants fall to the floor before stepping out of his shoes and socks, then finally tucked his thumbs under his boxers to reveal his thick, hard length.

God, I'd never tire of seeing him.

Unable to help myself, I scooted to the edge of the bed and motioned for him to come closer so I could grip his length and pull him into my mouth. Still, as I circled his tip with my tongue, I knew this wouldn't be enough. Not for a night like tonight. So, with hunger plain in my now husky voice, I looked up at him.

"Let's try it." I knew he understood what I meant, but he glanced down at me, a mischievous light in his eyes.

"Ah, love. Whatever you want. But let's get you nice and ready, then. Lay back for me."

I did as I was told, spreading my legs wide for him as he got on his knees in front of me and licked the space between my thighs.

By now, he knew my body like it was his own, loving every inch of me in all the ways he knew best. It was like every move was perfectly designed to inch me closer and closer to climax. As his calloused finger traced my folds, I writhed against him, willing him to end my torture and push inside me once and for all.

"I thought you wanted to . . ."

He looked up at me, a faint smile on his lips. "I do. I just want to make sure you enjoy it just as much as I will."

Without another word, he went back to work. My body squeezed around him while he sucked my clit and teased me relentlessly, pumping one finger into my pussy.

I whimpered, needing him to push in more. Just when I was near the point of pain, he pushed a second finger inside and I exploded, every bit of tension breaking apart into a million pieces. I cried out, gripping the covers as I screamed for Gavin, begging for more. When the rising swell of my pleasure finally slowed, he placed soft kisses against my thighs and spread my legs even further.

There was a silence, and then I felt something warm and slippery dripping down me. Gently, he massaged the lube into my skin, warming it as I rocked against his touch.

I couldn't deny that I was nervous, but as soon as I heard Gavin's voice, all my anxiety melted away.

"How are you feeling?"

"A little nervous. But excited too," I said, and it was true. For all the worry I felt, I was also curious. I wanted to know what this would feel like, but more than that, I wanted to be with him in every way I possibly could. Wanted to please him in every way.

"I'm going to get you ready now," he said. "If there's anything I do that you don't like, say stop and I will."

I nodded.

"Turn over for me," he whispered, helping me from

the spot where I lay so that I was now on my hands and knees.

"Good." He spanked me for good measure and then trailed his fingers up and down my backside, smoothing more liquid into the space before—I gasped—his other hand found my clit again and swirled in light, teasing circles.

"Relax, baby," he said.

I let out another gasp as a finger slid slowly but steadily into me. Into the place where I'd denied him all the times before. It was tight but not unpleasant, and he moved in and out slowly, readying me for more as his other hand worked its magic.

"Do you like that?" he asked.

"Yes," I hissed, and it was the truth. The curiosity in me grew and I arched, wanting to feel more, needing to please him.

"Good," he said, and then pushed another finger inside me.

Chapter Twenty-Four

Gavin

When Emma had murmured those three little words—*let's try it*—I knew exactly what she was asking for. My heart sprang into my throat, and I murmured something about needing to ready her first.

Though our last few days had been filled with exceptional amounts of nudity and hot sex, nothing could have prepared me for this moment. The diamond ring glinting on Emma's ring finger and her enthusiastic yes to my proposal make it all the sweeter. I felt stripped bare, flayed open in the best way possible. And now she was offering me her sweet virgin ass, all because she knew it was something I wanted.

Fuck.

Maybe that made me sick and twisted instead of a romantic—but, Christ, that did something to me.

As I watched her naked on the bed before me, it took every ounce of my self-control to slow myself down to make sure this would be good for her.

Go slow, Gavin.

Gripping her hips, I turned her over, my hands anchoring her ass high in the air. Emma supported her weight on her knees and forearms. She was so beautiful—fuck, her little pink asshole looked so tight and inviting—and I couldn't wait to take her there. But first, I had to make sure I wouldn't hurt her.

"I want you," Emma said softly, and I knew she was telling the truth. The way her body arched into my touch made my cock ache, but I forced myself to remain calm.

"Not yet, pet," I said, swirling my finger around her clit in the way I knew she would like, a little reward for her eagerness.

Before we went to the next level, I had to make absolutely certain she was ready for me. I didn't want to hurt her, and so I squirted more lube onto her, loving the way it dripped down her backside before I caught it and massaged it into her skin.

She let out a little moan and my cock throbbed again, wanting to be inside her already.

"You'll tell me if I hurt you?" I managed through gritted teeth. God, I hoped I was right, that she was enjoying this, because my cock was already aching and ready to burst.

She nodded.

My fingers continued moving inside, readying her, and her lips parted in surprise, though she showed no sign of pain.

We continued that way for the next several minutes until she glanced at me from over her shoulder, her eyes dark with lust. Withdrawing my fingers from her ass, I met her gaze, watching as her tongue wetted her bottom lip.

"You want this?" I asked, my fist wrapped around my swollen cock.

She nodded.

"Come and get it."

As I knelt on the bed behind her, Emma pressed her bottom back toward me, rubbing herself along the length of my erection, working her hips up and down, teasing me with her ass in a way that was so goddamn sexy.

Making sure to keep petting her wet cunt, I used my

other hand to grip my shaft and align myself between her cheeks. Ever so slowly, I began to push into her, inch by slow inch.

"Take a deep breath for me," I said, but she didn't need the direction. Instead, she let out a long, slow moan, her muscles relaxing around me as I pushed deeper and deeper inside her.

"Fuck yes." My voice sounded strained and far away. She was so tight. So hot. So perfect, and she was letting me do naughty, vile things to her.

My cock twitched at the sound of her tiny whimpers, and I gripped her hip, wanting to anchor myself inside her. "You like that, don't you?"

She arched her back in response. "So much. So, so much."

"Good girl," I said, my eyes sinking closed from the pleasure as I finally buried myself to the hilt, loving the warm, tight feel of her. Her ass was strangling my cock—and I fucking loved it.

Slowly, I began to thrust, moving in and out in short,

easy bursts at first, and then when she was pushing back against me, in longer, deeper strokes. With every move, she met me with enthusiasm and need, pushing me to work her faster, to stroke her harder, to show her my love more fiercely.

I'd waited patiently for this moment, and now that it was here, I didn't want to rush it. I wanted to stay inside her warm heat forever. Instead, we pushed each other closer to the edge, moaning together as our bodies found a rhythm we couldn't deny.

But I knew Emma, and I knew she couldn't hold back for long.

"You getting close?" I asked.

Nodding, she moaned. "Need you."

Folding my body over hers, I pressed my chest against the graceful curve of her back. Skin to skin. Heat to heat. "You have me."

As I dropped soft kisses down the slope of her spine, my hips continued thrusting, my cock taking her ass with everything I had now. I continued playing with her pussy, wanting her to feel the blinding pleasure I was experiencing.

"I want to feel you come," I managed to say.

That was all the invitation she needed. She arched her back, resting her cheek across her arms folded on the pillow, allowing me the most beautiful view of her body laid out before me, and then she let out a gasp like I'd never heard before.

"Fuck! Gavin!" She shrieked as she buried her face in the pillow, gripping the bedding while her body clenched wildly around me.

I closed my eyes, loving the hot, tight feel of her as her body quaked, and I worked her harder, faster, all the while listening to her whimpers of pleasure. It was like her orgasm stretched on for days, weeks, years, crashing in wave after wave of ecstasy until it finally slowed. I joined her, gripping her hips hard as I slammed into her body in hard, deep thrust after hard, deep thrust.

Closing my eyes, I savored the throb of my cock as I finished, loving the way my tension unraveled and burst apart inside my chest, tingling at the base of my spine, making my balls draw up as I emptied myself inside her tight ass.

"Holy fuck," I murmured, pulling out, utterly spent. I helped Emma to her side where she curled, watching me curiously.

"You . . . liked that, didn't you?"

Understatement of the year. "I think my cock's in love with your ass."

At this, she giggled, and I leaned over her to press a kiss to her lips. "Did you enjoy it?"

I didn't have to ask, I'd felt how hard she'd come, but I needed to hear her say the words. The idea of not knowing how she felt, if I'd accidentally hurt her—it would kill me.

"I didn't expect to, honestly. But yes, it was different . . . in a good way. In a hot-and-dirty kind of way."

I kissed her again. "You were amazing. Thank you for trusting me with that."

"I love you, Gavin," she murmured softly, her gaze warm and hazy.

"I love you a million billion," I told her, using the sweet words she'd murmured before.

• • •

After a shower and some cuddling, the rest of the night went on like that, making love and waiting until we could make love again. I couldn't even remember when or how we fell asleep. All I knew was that one moment I had Emma in my arms, her breasts bouncing as she rode me, and the next I was lying in my bed, my arm over my face to block out the morning sun.

If it weren't for the smell of bacon, I might have stayed there all morning. But then Emma was at my side with a plate of food and a cup of coffee, a wide grin on her face.

"Good morning, sleepyhead."

I cleared my throat. "Morning, my sweet fiancée."

Her face lit up with a smile. "I thought I'd dreamed last night, but when I woke up and saw your ring on my finger . . ." She held out her hand, inspecting the diamond that glinted in the light, and the rest of her words died on her lips.

"Last night was incredible," I said as I dragged myself to sit up.

"I agree." She winked. "I brought you some food to get your strength up."

I grinned and took a strip of bacon. "Very thoughtful of you."

Emma leaned closer and pressed a soft kiss to my lips.

"You're not sore, are you?" I murmured.

She shook her head, giving me a sassy smirk. "Nothing I can't handle. Even though your cock is fucking huge."

"Ha!" I couldn't help the laugh that burst from my lips. I brought her mouth to mine again and stole another kiss. "Mmm, you taste like bacon. Come back to bed."

"You can't possibly be ready to have sex again. We did it like sixty-nine times last night." Her tone was exasperated but her lips were curved into a smile.

"Sixty-nine?"

Dirty Little Promise 355

She rolled her eyes. "Don't get any ideas." Then she handed me my cell phone. "We have work to do. Your phone was ringing earlier."

Looking down, I noticed three missed calls and one message—two from my lawyer, and two from the judge on my case.

Trying to remain calm, I glanced at Emma. "I've got to listen to this. Can you give me a minute?"

"Of course." She nodded and then walked from the room as I pressed the phone to my ear to listen to the most recent message.

"Mr. Kingsley, this is Judge Reed. After reviewing the information in your case, I felt it was important to let you know that this won't be going any further. My office has been bombarded with letters from people informing me of the nature of your relationship with Ashley Stevens. And as a client of yours, I was also aware of your interactions with this young woman. This proceeding is a cash grab with no foundation, and after doing some digging, we found that the paperwork was filed incorrectly. This will be off the docket by Monday."

The message ended, and I stared at my phone for a

long moment before calling Emma back into the room.

She looked at me with wild eyes, a spatula in her hand. "What? What's wrong?"

When I told her what the message had said, she reeled back.

"Are you serious?"

I nodded. "Now, come here. I have some plans for what we can do with that spatula."

Chapter Twenty-Five

Emma

We decided on a winter wedding.

I wanted our ceremony to be in the library since it had inspired me so much. Not my tiny little suburban branch, but the big, beautiful library downtown. It gave me the chance to decorate the place I'd always felt was magical with a blizzard of paper snowflakes and fairy lights the way I'd always seen it in my imagination.

And that was exactly what we did. Surrounded by history and books and family, I walked down the aisle a few weeks later on my father's arm and married the man of my dreams, right there in the classical-poetry section. The wedding party was small—just Bethany in a plum-colored gown and Quinn in a matching bow tie and vest, but I barely saw any of it.

I only had eyes for Gavin.

He stood there waiting for me in his black tuxedo, and when I finally reached him, he held me close, whispering sweet things in my ear.

"You look stunning, Mrs. Kingsley."

At this, I thanked him, pressing a kiss to his freshly shaven cheek. But Gavin wasn't done.

"I never thought I'd have this moment, never thought I'd have anything close to this. I love you so much, baby."

"I love you a million billion," I whispered, stepping into position when the officiant cleared his throat.

The ceremony was short and sweet. We exchanged traditional vows, though it was likely the only part of our relationship that was traditional. And then, when the ceremony was over and I was in Gavin's arms, I felt so happy and fulfilled that I didn't know what to do with myself. All I knew was that with him by my side, everything was going to be okay.

At our reception, I was in Gavin's arms again, pressed to his chest as we swayed on the dance floor.

"Are you happy, wife?" he asked, a smirk on his lips.

"I'm so incredibly happy. I love you, Gavin."

As the music sped up to something faster, Gavin pressed a kiss to my mouth and led me back to the table.

Bethany sat there with her face in her hands, looking at us dreamily.

"Have I mentioned how gorgeous you look tonight?" he asked me.

"Only a thousand times." I smiled.

"Every time, it's been true." He touched one of the curls that framed my face.

"Are you sure you're not sad?"

He frowned. "You're my wife. What on earth would I have to be sad about now?"

I tried not to bring up the topic, as I knew it was a sore one for both Gavin and me. Last I'd heard, Cooper was living in Florida, doing God knows what. He hadn't followed through on the idea of opening a second location of Forbidden Desires, and I wasn't sure the reason, but I tried not to pry too much. It wasn't exactly a sore subject between Gavin and me, and yet it wasn't something I was entirely comfortable bringing up.

I bit my bottom lip. "You know, that Cooper isn't here."

Gavin and I hadn't discussed it when Cooper's RSVP card was never returned. We hadn't known what to expect today. Or, at least, we wouldn't admit what we knew in our hearts.

"No," Gavin said. "I'm not sad. Cooper has to find his way. And I think seeing you in your beautiful dress would have killed him all over again."

I nodded in agreement. Maybe it was for the best.

After dinner, my mother came by our table and pulled me away for a few minutes of girl talk. I was suspicious, but followed her.

"Are you guys going to start trying right away for a baby or wait a while?" my mother asked, bringing one arm around my shoulders as we wandered toward the balcony doors where a thousand stars twinkled outside in the night sky.

"Mom!"

She was being ridiculous. We'd only been husband and wife a matter of hours. Plus, Gavin and I hadn't had that conversation yet—about children. Maybe that was odd, but I'd always felt in my heart that I would be a

Dirty Little Promise 361

mother, and if I knew Gavin, there was nothing he'd deny me.

"It's not something I've thought about much, Mom," I admitted.

She nodded. "Fine. Just enjoy your new husband. But don't make me wait too long to become a grandma."

With my mom's words ringing in my ears, I greeted relatives and chatted with friends I hadn't seen since college. Gavin was the perfect gentleman, kind and funny, and he handled my drunk uncle Byron beautifully. I could barely keep my eyes off him, my new husband. I didn't think I'd ever tire of that word.

Later, he pulled me to the dance floor again, and I melted against his firm, broad chest. We swayed to the music with our family and friends looking on.

"Can I ask you something?" I said.

"Hmm?"

"I know it's early. We've only been married three hours, but . . ."

"What is it?" His brows drew together and he paused in the center of the dance floor.

"Actually, you know what? Let's go get a drink." I gave his hand a tug, but Gavin remained rooted in place.

"As long as you promise to tell me what's on your mind, pet."

Wishing I'd never brought it up, I reluctantly agreed with a nod.

Back at our table with glasses of fresh champagne in front of us, Gavin leaned close. "Tell me."

"I've been thinking about our future."

"And?" he asked, clearly unsure about where this conversation was heading.

God, why was this so difficult? I took a deep breath. Gavin was my husband. I could tell him anything. We hadn't discussed having children yet, but I knew in my heart he wouldn't deny me anything. If I wanted to be a mother, I felt sure he'd support that.

"Do you want kids?" I asked.

His mouth pulled into a frown. "I'm not sure this is the best place for us to have this conversation."

My heart sank. His tone was harsh and unhappy, like I'd just asked to perform a colonoscopy on him in public.

"I see."

"Are you surprised, Emma? I'm not the fatherly type. Given my childhood, and what I do for a living? There's no way I'd want to bring a child into this world. Not ever."

Tears stinging my eyes, I quickly excused myself and headed for the bathroom.

God, I felt so foolish. Why hadn't I ever thought to bring this up with him before?

A short time later, Gavin found me standing beside the dance floor with my mother, and he laced his fingers with mine. "Please forgive me. Let's talk about it later."

I nodded, my throat tight. Drawing in a deep breath, I tried to force the thoughts out of my mind. I had to have faith that we'd figure it all out later.

We had to.

• • •

And then somehow, it was after midnight and the reception was ending. It had all gone by so fast, I wanted nothing more than to press rewind and do the whole thing again.

I hugged my parents and said good-bye to the few last lingering guests before Gavin crossed the room, tucking me close to his side.

"Will you forgive me, wife? We can talk about your proposal again another time," he whispered in a low voice.

I nodded and forced the thoughts of babies from my brain. I wouldn't let anything ruin my wedding night—not even this uncertainty that hung around us like a cloud. Gavin was my husband now, my everything, and maybe that would have to be enough.

We said our good-byes to our guests before climbing into the limo to head home. Once inside the limo, I slid off my heels and let out a heavy sigh.

"Tonight was incredible, wasn't it?"

Gavin watched me with hooded eyes. "It was perfect.

But I'm a very conflicted man."

"Why's that?"

"Because I want you to wear that dress forever, but I also want to tear it off of you."

I smiled as we pulled up in front of my brownstone. I hadn't been back to the place except to grab a few of my things, but based on the huge red bow on the door, I had to guess the renovations were complete.

"Gavin?" I asked as we stepped out of the limo.

"Come see."

We made our way through the door, and I gasped.

It was like stepping back in time. Every single thing inside was how my grandmother had had it. Every piece of furniture looked genuine, polished, and perfect. Tears sprang to my eyes but I wiped them away, desperate to drink in as much of the wonderful changes as I could.

"I know you're not ready to part with this place, that it's part of you. You can do with it whatever you wish. Have girls' night here. Use it as a hideout when I act like an asshole."

I laughed, the sound full and light. "I know what I want to do. I want to open a bookstore here."

"I think it's a brilliant plan."

After we had toured the home with all its beautiful renovations, we were soon back in the limo and I was in Gavin's lap, kissing him deeply.

"Let's go home," I murmured. "I need you."

"So, have me." Gavin gave me a wicked smile but I shook my head.

"I'm not riding you wearing a wedding dress while Ben watches."

Gavin chuckled. "Probably a good call. He's a good employee, and I wouldn't want to have to kill him."

And then we were home—in our bed—all tangled limbs and urgent kisses. We made love slowly, so achingly slow and tender.

But as amazing as it was, a little spot inside my chest still hurt at Gavin's refusal to make a baby with me.

Dirty Little Promise

Epilogue

Emma

We'd adjusted to living together with only a few minor bumps in the road. Gavin was a neat freak and employed a housekeeper who came twice a week to do all the cleaning and laundry. I joked that that fact alone was worth marrying him for.

His sexual appetite for me hadn't cooled, not that I'd wanted it to. The fact that he needed me pretty much daily—that he couldn't seem to pass me by in the hall without stealing a kiss—it made me feel incredibly wanted. Incredibly loved and cherished.

We alternated cooking and ordering takeout, and generally figured out a simple system that worked best for us. My favorite was the quiet nights we spent in the media room, sharing a ten-dollar pizza and a sixty-dollar bottle of wine while cuddled together on the couch.

When we first announced our engagement and then our wedding date just a few weeks later, it had been difficult to convince our friends and family I wasn't pregnant. From our first date to our wedding day was only three and a half months. But when you knew, you just knew.

This was no shotgun wedding. My affections for Gavin had begun almost a year before we officially met, so to us, of course, it felt like much longer. A year of an unrequited crush, a year of yearning—it was a long time. And we were done waiting. It was a whirlwind engagement, but we wanted to spend every night together, to wake up together every morning. He was my other half, and his presence made me feel whole.

By Christmastime, when I wasn't "showing" and was still drinking an occasional glass of wine, Bethany and my mother were forced to finally ease up about the whole baby thing.

But I didn't want to think about that right now, didn't want to think about the conversation about kids I'd forced onto Gavin the night of our wedding. We would figure it out and navigate it in our own way, just like we did everything else. I had to have faith—the alternative was just too grim—and it was Christmas, time to be festive and happy.

Pushing those thoughts from my brain, I turned toward the full-length mirror again, hurrying to get ready for the ugly-Christmas-sweater party we were attending at Forbidden Desires tonight.

I knew Gavin was going to appreciate the black silk stockings and black Christian Louboutin heels he'd gotten me. He hadn't even said anything; they'd just appeared. But he was always doing things like that lately, ordering me wonderful gifts online, or picking up things he thought I'd like in cute little boutiques on his way home from the office.

Sometimes, for no reason at all, silky lingerie would arrive in a gift box. A designer handbag was delivered the day after I complained about the straps on my old purse fraying. My favorite, by far, was a vintage book of poetry that showed up at the breakfast table.

And then tonight, I found my new sexy, daring heels sitting on the ivory-colored tufted bench at the end of our bed with a note in Gavin's neat handwritten scrawl.

Wife,

Wear these for me tonight?

— *G*

I couldn't refuse him. The shoes were exquisite, but paired with my ugly Christmas sweater? The effect was more comical than sexy.

I arranged my long hair over my shoulders, hoping that would hide some of the hideousness, and strutted from the bathroom, trying to own my new look. No one at the party could fault me for not trying, because the dancing green and red drunken elves across my chest were proof of my level of commitment to tonight's festivities.

"Gavin?" I called, rounding the corner to the living room. I found him standing near the fireplace, reading the Christmas card my parents had sent. Every year, they wrote a lengthy Christmas letter to all their friends and family, and this year's included their bliss at their only daughter's marriage to a Mr. Gavin Kingsley. It still warmed my heart to think about how they had accepted him into the fold, despite their initial reservations.

"Fuck," he said gruffly when he looked up.

I tugged on my miniskirt again. "I look stupid, don't

I?"

He placed the card back on the mantel before turning to face me again. He stalked toward me with calculated steps, not stopping until he'd wandered around behind me, appraising me from every angle.

"You look stunning."

"Gavin?" I said in a warning voice when he stopped to face me.

My heart rate accelerated because I knew that look in his eye. It was one that said he wanted to dominate and control, and fuck me until I was a gasping mess. And I also knew that our friends and family were waiting on us. My parents would be there, for heaven's sake.

He wasn't wearing an ugly Christmas sweater, but then again, he was Gavin fucking Kingsley. I'd never expected him to. Instead, he was dressed in a pair of perfectly tailored dark jeans, low suede boots, a crisp white button-down shirt, and the tie I'd gotten him as a compromise. It was hunter green with little red Christmas trees all over it. The effect was actually quite adorable, and I melted a little inside.

He stroked my cheek, his eyes still molten and adoring.

"You wore it," I murmured.

"Of course I did."

• • •

Gavin

"Take off your skirt and panties," I said, my voice resolute.

Emma hesitated, lifting her delicate chin to meet my steely gaze. "But we'll be late for the party."

I stalked closer. "Don't make me repeat myself."

For a moment, I didn't think she'd obey. It would have been a first—but then she reached beneath her leather miniskirt and drew a pair of lacy black panties down to her knees. When they dropped to her slim ankles, she rested a hand on my shoulder, supporting her weight as she carefully stepped out of them, making sure they didn't get tangled in the lovely stiletto heels she wore.

Next came the hiss of the zipper on the back of her skirt as she lowered it. Then Emma was standing before me with her bare cunt, her mouthwatering cunt, and wearing nothing but black silk stockings and heels with that ridiculous fucking ugly Christmas sweater.

I knew she felt a little strange and highly exposed, and that was what I wanted. I'd use her uncertainty to test her limits, to push her to new levels of pleasure.

Releasing my belt with a swift tug, I unbuttoned my jeans and drew down my zipper, freeing all nine inches of my hard dick. Her gaze fell to my groin, and Emma sucked in a sharp inhale as two bright spots of color appeared high on her cheeks.

Her body and all its reactions were an aphrodisiac to me.

"Do you see what you do to me?" I hissed, sounding angrier than I actually felt.

Emma didn't respond.

"I thought being married was supposed to calm you down, that it would make me docile and relaxed. Instead, I get hard every time you walk into the room, and I want you more with each passing day. I want to make you cry out in pleasure, to watch you lose yourself, to know that it's me and *only me* you come for."

"Yes," she said softly, sagging against my chest.

"What was that, sweet wife?" I whispered near her ear.

Emma straightened, meeting my eyes. "Yes, *sir*."

Bringing my hand between her legs, I stroked her once, so slowly, savoring how soft and warm she felt. And smirking at the fact that she was already wet.

"Is that for me?" I asked, teasing her slick skin. It was soft. So heavenly soft, and I wanted to lose myself in her. To push inside and never leave. But, first things first. I took a deep breath, composing myself.

Tossing my tie over one shoulder, I placed one hand firmly against her shoulder, encouraging her to sink to her knees before me.

Realizing that she rested on the hardwood floor, I sighed and coaxed her forward by taking a few steps back until we were on the plush living room rug. God, when had I become such a fucking softy? Falling in love would do that to a man, I supposed.

I was still fully dressed—my shirt buttoned to the throat, my leather shoes in a wide stance as I stood before her like a king. Only my cock was drawn out for her to pleasure me.

Emma wrapped me in her warm palm, and as good as it felt, the need for control clawed at me.

"Did I say you could use your hands?" I snapped.

She released my cock with a soft whimper, placing her hands behind her back as she brought her mouth to me instead.

"There. Just like that."

Feather-soft licks traced down the length of my shaft, stopping at my balls where she nuzzled into me, causing my breath to lodge in my throat.

Fuck.

I stroked the silky strands of her hair back from her face, watching her work and very much enjoying the show. She sucked me deeper, causing a groan to rip from my throat.

Jesus.

"Swallow that cock. Just like that."

Emma took me deeper still, flattening her tongue and gliding along my now glistening flesh.

"Good girl."

"Is this okay, sir?" Her tone was teasing. She knew damn well it was fucking incredible.

"You're doing fine. And maybe, if you can make me come," I glanced at my watch, "in the next four minutes, I'll reward you." The truth was, we were running late, but none of that mattered the moment Emma walked out of our bedroom looking the way she did.

She redoubled her efforts, her head bobbing, her tongue lapping, all while she made the most toe-curling wet sucking sounds against my dick. Those noises alone were enough to undo me.

After a couple of minutes watching her suck me off, the need for control flared inside me, making my palms itch. I needed to take over. Needed it almost as badly as I needed my next breath.

"Stay still," I ordered.

Emma stopped, her mouth open, waiting for my next command.

Placing my hands on either side of her face, I pushed forward, testing her. Emma let out a tiny moan. That was all the invitation I needed. Soon, I was thrusting my hips, fucking her throat in hard jabs—again and again—until my ass muscles clenched and I came in a loud grunt, my semen disappearing down her throat before she had the chance to pull away. Not that she would have.

"Well done, pet." I checked my watch again with a smirk before offering her a hand and helping her to her feet.

I led her to the kitchen island, her heels clicking across the wood floor as she followed. When we reached the marble island, I lifted her, sitting her right on top of it. She flinched at the chill of the stone against her bare ass.

"You okay?" I murmured.

Emma gave me a slight nod, her eyes on mine, her

pupils dilated with an equal mix of desire and uncertainty.

"You did such a nice job swallowing my cock, I'm going to let you come on my tongue. Would you like that, love?"

Emma blinked at me several times in quick succession. I wondered if she was about to argue again that we'd be late for the party, but then she gave a soft sigh and leaned back on her elbows, her knees parted in invitation.

I started slowly, bringing my mouth close to her, letting my breath ghost over her slick flesh.

She was pink and soft and all mine. Knowing she was my *wife*, that it was my ring on her finger, made it all the sweeter. Knowing that no man would ever touch her again, that it was solely my responsibility to cherish her and pleasure her was a heady feeling, and one I didn't take lightly. I would protect her always, would love her forever, and I'd make damn sure my bride was satisfied all the days of her life.

As I slid one finger inside her warm cunt, Emma released a soft whimper. My dick hardened again at the sound of her, at the sight of her taking her pleasure. Her hips rocked forward, and she shamelessly rubbed her pretty cunt all over my mouth.

Pulling back, I nibbled at her inner thigh, leaving soft bite marks against her skin. "Stay nice and still," I warned.

Emma obeyed, and I rewarded her by flattening my tongue and working her clit over at a frenzied pace.

"Gavin!" she cried out, already incredibly close.

As I pumped my fingers in and out, Emma trembled, her body tightening as her orgasm drew closer still. I ate her like she was my favorite meal, lapping up every last drop of the sweet honey she gave me.

"Give it to me," I murmured.

Emma came with a cry that was the sweetest song I'd ever heard. Afterward, she looked at me like she didn't know whether to thank me or return the favor.

When I fetched her clothes and helped her down from the counter, she redressed, supporting herself against me, still shaky in her heels, her cheeks flushed and pink.

I loved the blissful look on her face. She looked almost confused about what had transpired since she'd walked out of the bedroom, and it was fucking adorable.

"Are you ready to go see your parents?" I asked with a pleased smirk.

Emma nodded.

"Good." I helped her into her coat and we headed for the door.

On the ride down the elevator, I pulled Emma close, bringing my mouth to her neck.

"I love you a million billion," I whispered against her skin.

Her eyes flashed on mine, and a slow smile uncurled on her lips. "I love you a million billion," she whispered back.

My heart was so full, so full of her, of her love, I felt like anything was possible. She made me strong and brave and whole.

And I knew with certainty I'd love her until my dying breath.

"Let's go have some fun tonight," I said, and she grinned at me.

"Let's."

• • •

Emma

When we arrived at the office Christmas party, I was momentarily taken aback by the sight of so many beautiful women in one place. All these months, it had been easy to forget that Gavin ran an escort agency, but now? Not so much.

Gavin didn't release my hand as he led me into the office. And he didn't so much as glance at any of the women.

I stopped to hug Alyssa and waved to a couple of people I recognized, feeling calmer already. The invite list for their ugly-sweater party read like an enviable who's who of the Boston social scene. Politicians and notable members of the media were there, as well as a couple of professional athletes.

And then there were my parents, standing near the

punch bowl with wide eyes.

Oh dear God.

I prayed for their sake—and mine—that the eggnog was heavily spiked.

"Hey, Mom." Gavin greeted my mother, pulling her into a swift hug with an easy smile.

She beamed, patting his chest. "Don't you look handsome as ever, son."

"Hi, Mom," I said, giving her a hug.

I was perfectly okay with playing second fiddle to Gavin. It was sweet, their adoration and understanding for each other. To say that Gavin had won my mom over was the understatement of the year. They had a very cute and special relationship.

"Daddy." I grinned as I lifted up on my toes to press a kiss to his cheek.

"You two are late," my father said.

Gavin muttered an apology as he shook my father's hand.

"Are you guys enjoying yourselves?" I asked, feeling a little self-conscious. What I meant was, *Are you scarred for life?*

Gavin had insisted upon inviting them, taking this whole family thing seriously. He had parents in his life for the first time in a long time, and he was trying to make the most of it. I never thought they'd actually come, but they were trying to accept all the various sides and sometimes sharp angles to their new son-in-law, so I knew I shouldn't complain.

"It's been rather . . . enlightening," my mother said, her gaze darting to where a group of escorts in their twenties were doing shots at the bar.

My father nodded toward a white-haired man across the room. "Is that the CEO of Goldschmidt's bank over there?"

Gavin nodded. "He's been a client for years, actually. Good guy. I can introduce you later, if you like."

My father's face lit up like the Fourth of July. "That'd be terrific."

My mother pursed her lips. "Don't you even think about trading me in for one of these hot little numbers, Frank," she warned.

That answered the question about whether the eggnog was spiked. My mother's tongue was already loosened. *God help us all tonight.*

Dad put a loving arm around my mom's shoulders. "Wouldn't dream of it. I have everything I need right here." They shared a quick kiss while Gavin and I exchanged a look.

Gavin led my father over to meet his man crush, and Mom and I took our drinks to wander around and mingle. It hardly looked like their office with the low lighting, and all the furniture moved out of the way to accommodate a small bar and parquet dance floor.

I chuckled to see Quinn was dressed as Santa Claus, complete with a red velvet suit, stuffed belly, and white beard. His perfectly styled dark hair wasn't covered by a wig, though, so the effect was rather hilarious. He was a hot Santa, and he was truly the center of attention. With Gavin now married and Cooper nowhere to be found, that left the dozen or so escorts in the room focusing on

Quinn—sitting on his lap, pressing lipstick kisses to his cheek, and smiling at his every word.

For the first time, I realized how lonely it must be being Quinn Kingsley. As the oldest brother of the family, he had so much weight on his shoulders as he guided the ship. The smudge of dark circles under his eyes was faintly visible. While he was jovial tonight, all smiles and hearty laughs, I could tell it wasn't always that easy for him.

Pushing the somber thoughts away, I introduced my mom to Alyssa, and they struck up an easy conversation. As I stood there, enjoying the low pulse of electronic holiday music pumping through the speakers, my mind began to drift.

This year was so strange. It was Christmastime, but instead of baking cookies and stocking up on sweaters, I'd spent the morning picking out bikinis, modeling each one for Gavin in the department-store dressing room. Tomorrow, we'd leave for the vacation in the Seychelles islands Gavin had bid on and won at the charity gala we'd attended together earlier this year—fourteen days spent on a private yacht in the Indian Ocean off the coast of East Africa. A late honeymoon, a holiday getaway . . .

whatever you wanted to call it, it was my idea of heaven.

Of course, my parents had balked that I wouldn't be home for Christmas with my new husband. It amused me to think about Gavin sleeping in my childhood bedroom with me, probably tying me up with my old equestrian ribbons or making me wear my old cheerleading uniform while we made love. And, of course, I would have done it. It was impossible to deny Gavin something he wanted.

Traditions like that with my family would come later, in time. Their acceptance of Gavin, of us, meant the world to me. My mom had continued with her quest for grandbabies, reminding me that I'd be thirty next year.

I still wasn't sure what to make of Gavin's uncertainty about that subject, and tried to hide how worried I felt about it.

Later, my parents met Quinn, and while they chatted about my dad's favorite football team, Gavin turned toward me.

"Come with me," he said, taking my hand and drawing me into a private alcove in the office. "There's something I want to say to you."

My heart beat faster, stealing my breath. "Okay."

He brushed my hair lovingly from my face and took a step closer. "There were so many things I never thought I'd do. Fall in love, get married . . ."

He left it off the list, but I imagined having a falling-out with Cooper would have been on that list too. And that stung, because I knew it was my fault. It still made my heart hurt after all this time. But I couldn't focus on Cooper right now because Gavin was opening up, baring yet another piece of his soul to me, and I hung on his every word.

"What are you saying, Gavin?"

"I also never thought I'd be a father, but I've been thinking about it lately, thinking about what you said. Let's have a baby."

Suddenly breathless and at a complete loss for words, I felt my mouth curve into a suspicious smile. "What are you talking about?"

He shrugged, pulling me close to his chest. "Having all those things I never thought I'd want, they've taught me I can't be afraid to say yes to the good things in life. You've made me so happy, Emma. I want this too. With you."

"Gavin . . ." My heart surged with even more love for this man.

"What do you say, love?"

I brought my lips to his, kissing my silly, loving husband. "Of course I do. But, I'm sorry, I'm kind of in shock right now."

"Want to make a baby?" he asked, waggling his eyebrows.

"My bookstore isn't even open yet. I think we should wait a couple of months. I'll get off birth control, and we can figure out the right time."

He brought my hand to his lips, kissing the back of it. "Of course. There's no rush."

My heart swelled at the thought of Gavin with a baby, the thought of someone else, even a tiny creature, loving him so unconditionally. It made my heart feel incredibly full.

He might have thought he was doing this for me, but truly, this would be one of the biggest gifts and blessings in his life. He just didn't know it yet. Fatherhood would suit Gavin. I knew it.

He was commanding, yet loving. Firm, but fair. Guarded, but affectionate. I wasn't worried, not one single bit. And I almost laughed at the idea of how overprotective he'd be of me while I was pregnant. But if I could survive an over-the-top alpha male doting on me, I knew our happily-ever-after would be amplified tenfold.

"How many do you want?" I asked, still giddy and drunk on this conversation, and not wanting it to end.

He kissed me again, pulling back slowly. "I don't know. Three? Four?"

I barked out a laugh. "Whoa, overachiever. Let's start with one and go from there."

"Okay," he said, agreeing a little reluctantly.

Bringing my lips to his, I murmured, "You don't know how happy you've made me."

"I love you," he said softly, his lips still against mine.

"A million billion," I finished for him.

And then he swept me off my feet, carrying me toward his office down the hall where I imagined we'd do very naughty things.

Epilogue II

Cooper

My phone buzzed, and against my better judgment, I glanced down at the screen. It was Quinn. It was always Quinn these days.

Gavin never bothered contacting me anymore. Not that I could blame him. The rift between us had grown into something so vast and unmanageable, I didn't know how we'd ever climb our way out.

I didn't bother replying to my brother's message, because honestly? I didn't have an answer to his question. I didn't know when I was going home. Being surrounded by palm trees and ocean breezes suited me just fine right now. And the girls with their sun-kissed shoulders and bikini lines were working overtime to keep me distracted.

Boston would always be my home, and my business was there. While I knew I'd have to return eventually, I wasn't in any rush.

"Who was that?" the blonde crouched between my thighs asked.

"Did I tell you to stop?" I frowned down at her.

She bit her lip, watching me through heavily made-up eyes.

"Suck my cock. Make me come." Those were the words I said, but the words I meant were *make me forget*.

The naked blonde kneeling in front me went back to work, tasting the broad head of my cock before drawing it deeper into her mouth.

"That's it, princess."

I called every girl *princess* now. The word stung the first few times leaving my lips, which was all the more reason to use it. The need to work Emma out from under my skin was immense. And what better way to cast her memory away than to pretend she never existed. She wasn't my princess, and neither were any of the others.

And I was no prince—I was just a lonely bachelor who used to believe in love.

But these days, I was done being the nice guy. It hadn't gotten me anywhere. And women, it turned out, wanted the asshole. My experiment with Gavin had proven that. And no, I wasn't going to *pretend* to be an asshole simply because I was willing to play the part.

Sweet little Emma Bell had actually turned me into one.

She had broken me.

I hated to admit defeat, but Emma fucking Bell—excuse me, Emma Kingsley now—had turned me into a shell of the man I once was.

It was my own fault. I'd known from the beginning that I was playing with fire, knew she'd be perfect for my brother and had done my best to push them together. And the thing was, I was actually happy for the motherfucker. But that didn't mean it didn't hurt like hell to see them together.

Now it was my rules, my way.

"Is this how you like it?" the blonde asked, seeming to sense my distant thoughts.

I tilted my head back, closing my eyes. "Deeper."

Losing myself in the pleasure, in the wet, lapping heat of her tongue, I tried to push everything else from my brain. I had no plans to return home, no plans to do anything other than this—get drunk and take home a different woman, night after night. This would be my life. No, it wouldn't be rich, or deep, or all that fulfilling, but it was what I had. What I deserved now.

My phone rang again, this time with Gavin's name, and my stomach clenched. *Fucking Gavin.* What could he possibly want?

The realization that I'd be heading back to Boston much sooner than anticipated settled over me like a dark cloud, and I steeled myself for what was to come.

Up Next in the Forbidden Desires Series
Torrid Little Affair

The best way to get over someone is to get under someone else. And I have the perfect candidate all picked out.

My new assistant is tempting beyond belief with her curvy body and take-no-shit attitude. All those luscious curves, and a juicy ass I'm already in love with. God, the things that I would do to that ass…

But it's the haunted look in her eyes that speaks to me. Like she's taken just as much shit in her past as I have—maybe more. We both deserve a little fun. Love can't fix everything. Mind-blowing sex and a few killer orgasms, on the other hand?

I have a feeling those might do the trick.

This is book three in the Forbidden Desires series, and while it can be read as a standalone, it's recommended you start with Dirty Little Secret.

Also in This Series

Dirty Little Secret

Torrid Little Affair

Tempting Little Tease

Naughty Little Scandal

Acknowledgments

A massive thank-you to the following people for helping this story come to life:

First, to my amazing publicist and right hand in all things, Danielle Sanchez. When I mentioned this story idea I had for three brothers who owned an escort agency, and you said, "Ohhh, you should write that next," your enthusiasm was the reason I did.

Author Rachel Brookes, thank you for believing in my alpha asshole brothers, and for loving this story. It means the world.

Thank you to GoodReads diva extraordinaire Sue Bee for taking the time to beta read this book. Your feedback and guidance helped tremendously. I was so happy when the queen of fictional alpha males told me that I had nailed Gavin, and that his hot-and-cold personality was perfect.

For Natasha Madison, thank you for loving everything I write.

A huge thank-you to Sarah Hansen for my lovely covers for this series, and to Michelle Tan for designing such beautiful graphics.

To Alyssa Garcia, you deal with my crazy on a daily basis, and I'm so thankful to have you as my executive assistant. It only seemed right to name Gavin's assistant after you.

Thank you to all the wonderful reviewers, bloggers, librarians, booksellers, and readers who requested early review copies. We were overwhelmed by your excitement for this series.

A huge tackle-hug and a glass of fizzy champagne to all the readers who waited patiently for book two. You are the reason I get to continue bringing my stories to life, and I truly hope you loved this one as much as I did. I can't wait to bring you more in the story, including more books about Cooper, Quinn, and a naughty little surprise in book five that's already shaping up to be my favorite.

About the Author

A *New York Times*, *Wall Street Journal*, and *USA TODAY* bestselling author of more than two dozen titles, Kendall Ryan has sold over two million books, and her books have been translated into several languages in countries around the world. Her books have also appeared on the *New York Times* and *USA TODAY* bestseller list more than three dozen times. Ryan has been featured in publications such as *USA TODAY*, *Newsweek*, and *In Touch Magazine*. She lives in Texas with her husband and two sons.

Website: www.kendallryanbooks.com

Other Books by Kendall Ryan

Unravel Me

Make Me Yours

Working It

When I Break Series

Filthy Beautiful Lies Series

The Gentleman Mentor

Sinfully Mine

Bait & Switch

Slow & Steady

The Room Mate

The Play Mate

The House Mate

The Soul Mate

Hard to Love

Reckless Love

Resisting Her

The Impact of You

Screwed

Monster Prick

The Fix Up

Sexy Stranger

Dirty Little Secret

Printed in Great Britain
by Amazon